AF487703

WHEN OUTLAWS RULED

ABE DELANEY AND TRACKER
BOUNTY HUNTERS

ORRIS SLADE

Copyright © 2021 by Orris Slade.

All rights reserved. No part of this publication may be reproduced, distributed or transmitted in any form or by any means, including photocopying, recording, or other electronic or mechanical methods, without the prior written permission of the publisher, except in the case of brief quotations embodied in critical reviews and certain other noncommercial uses permitted by copyright law.

Publisher's Note: This is a work of fiction. Names, characters, places and incidents are a product of the author's imagination. Locales and public names are sometimes used for atmospheric purposes. Any resemblance to actual people, living or dead, or to businesses, companies, events, institutions, or locales is completely coincidental.

Contents

Prologue

July 1880

Fort Keating, Texas

Bang! Bang! Bang!

Shards of glass rained down on Abraham Delaney as he reloaded. Four shot were fired in rapid succession. Each hit the wall just inches beside his head, punctuated by a dark puff of gunpowder that stained the outlaw's fingers. Abe peered around the wall peppered with bullet holes and caught sight of bandits robbing the bank. Two masked men pinned Abe and Tracker down with gunfire, a hogtied security guard at their feet. Another bandit kept his gun trained on the customers, while his partner forced the bank tellers to their knees behind the counter. The final bandit, the leader, gripped the bank manager by the back of his neck and steered him into the room with the large safe and lock boxes.

Tracker brushed the glass and debris from his shoulder before he gestured toward the two guards with a flick of his wrist. Abe didn't need Tracker to use words. They had worked together long enough they could practically read each other's minds. He followed Tracker's lead and leapt out from behind the wall, pulling the trigger as he dashed toward a table near the teller's counter. Tracker used the distraction to disarm one guard. Abe crawled beneath the table and kicked open a pair of large wooden doors. The hostages ran from the bank, screaming out for help as Abe dodged bullets that came his way.

A bandit cursed loudly and lunged for Abe's throat. The bounty hunter sidestepped the attack, causing the bandit to stumble. He reared his arm back and pummeled the man with his fist. Pain exploded across his ribcage as the bandit rammed his knee into Abe's side. Abe rolled them over before knocking his opponent unconscious with a vicious blow to the head. He gasped for breath, panting heavily, just before a second bandit grabbed him from behind. He dragged Abe across the floor, scraping his back across the rubbish on the ground. He called out for Tracker, and his partner tossed a knife into the air. It spun with a whistle, and the bandit with Abe in his grasp dropped with a loud thud.

Abe jumped to his feet with a pained groan. He grabbed the chair beside the teller's counter and smashed it over one of the masked men's back. When the bandit fell to his knees, Abe kneed him in the face, breaking his nose.

"I'll take care of the last one," Tracker shouted. "Get the hostage."

He nodded to his partner and crept along the wall toward the door to the backroom. Boots tapped softly against the polished wood floors as he stepped over bullet casings and chunks of splintered wood that littered the ground, careful not to alert the leader to his approach. Sweat slithered down his temple before it dripped along the curve of his throat and soaked into the collar of his shirt. Muffled voices drifted from beneath the door as he eased open the iron gate that protected the safe.

Abe spotted the bandit near the lock boxes.

The safe had already been emptied. Most bandits would have filled the bags and headed out the back by now, but Abe knew the leader of the bank robbers was a man with gold and jewels on his mind.

"Open the lock boxes!" the bandit barked. "Don't try nothin' foolish."

The bank manager trembled in fear, the muzzle of a shotgun pressed between his shoulder blades. "Only the owners of the lock boxes can access them. They require a special key that is unique to each lock."

Abe stepped into the flickering light of the oil lamp on the desk in the room. He heard the shotgun cock and clenched his jaw. "You should have taken the money and headed for the hills, friend," he scoffed. "Lower the gun, nice and slow, and maybe you can walk out of here in one piece. Nobody else needs to get hurt."

The bandit moved behind the bank manager, placing the hostage between Abe and himself. The cowardice of criminals never failed to surprise Abe. He curled his lip as the man spoke, "Ain't no way I'm doin' that, mister."

Abe shrugged his shoulders, keeping his grip firm on the gun. "Your crew has already been taken care of," he replied gruffly. "Right now, my partner has all of them wrapped up like a gift for the sheriff. I would surrender if I were you. All the noise will draw attention."

"Who are you?" The bandit glanced between Abe and the bank manager nervously. "You some sort of lawman?"

"I was just passing through," he sighed. "Saw a few unsavory characters acting suspicious and just followed my gut." Abe stepped lightly as he moved away from the door.

As expected, the bandit mirrored his movements and positioned himself in front of the lock boxes. Abe struck immediately. He knocked over the lamp, forcing the bandit to release the hostage unless he wanted to catch fire, and shot the lock box directly behind the masked gunman. The bullet ricocheted off the metal face of the lock box and struck the bandit in the hip. Abe shoved the bank manager out of the room just before the shotgun bucked in the bandit's hand.

Tracker burst inside the back room, gun drawn and aimed at the bandit on the floor as he made his way over to Abe's side. "Is that all of them?" he asked.

Abe returned his firearm to its holster and braced his hands on his knees. Each heaving breath that was dragged into his lungs echoed in the small room. None of the lock boxes had been opened, and the bags of money sat on the desk just a few feet away from Abe. The bounty hunter smiled up at Tracker with a hint of cockiness in his expression. "For now," he chuckled. "But who knows what tomorrow will bring?"

A strange look eclipsed the relief Abe saw in his partner's eyes, and the sound of a hammer being pulled back on a rifle rang in his ears. The heat from the muzzle burned his cheek as a sixth bandit appeared, as if out of thin air.

Chapter 1

August 1880

En Route to San Antonio, Texas

A falcon's screech pierced the air. Hooves pounded against the dirt road that cut through the valley as the wagon rolled alongside two deputies and a Texas Ranger. The men were on edge. Ivan "the Reaper" Lincoln could practically smell the stench of fear that wafted off the lawmen. A cruel smile curled on his lips, for he knew his name alone had haunted the minds of every man in the west.

The second signal came as the wagon veered down the path that led to the city.

It was time.

Ivan nodded to his right-hand man, Victor, and both outlaws gripped the side of the wagon. The shackles around their wrists and ankles jingled as they used all their strength to rock the wagon back and forth. Ivan heard the Texas Ranger shout for the men to stop the transport. But it was too late. They gave one last push, and the world turned upside down. The chains jerked painfully on Ivan's limbs as the wagon tumbled off the path.

A cloud of dirt blew into Ivan's face. He coughed and sputtered, holding on for dear life as the wagon continued to roll. Unyielding metal clasps rubbed against the tender skin of his wrists, causing them to bleed. Ivan gritted his teeth and pressed his feet against the floor of the wagon just as it slid to a stop. Already, he could hear approaching hooves, so he had to work quickly. He pulled on the shackles with a white-knuckled grip until the bolt securing their chains to the wagon snapped. Ivan and Victor flopped onto their backs on top of the wagon cover.

They scrambled to their feet in a hurry. Victor whistled loudly, and three riders approached the overturned wagon. Jasper hopped down from his saddle with a blacksmith's cutter in his hand. Ivan lifted his arms out toward the other outlaw and breathed a sigh of relief when the shackles fell to the ground. He rubbed his wrists as he glanced over his shoulder at the Texas Ranger who rode toward them with a burning hatred in his eyes.

Ivan walked over to the lawmen as four more riders appeared. That cruel smile returned to his face when the deputies were snatched from their horses before they knew what was happening. Though his crew was smaller than most gangs, it was made up of the most hated outlaws in Texas. Arson, murder, robbery… nothing was too wicked for Ivan and his crew. He wiped the blood from his hands as the lawmen were dragged over and forced to their knees in front of him.

"Texas is a land of opportunity," Ivan muttered in his polished accent that often turned heads in the south. "There are acres of wilderness that are still unclaimed, lands that expand as far as the eye can see. It's what separates the civility of the east and the untamed west."

The Texas Ranger glared up at Ivan before the outlaw slammed his fist against the lawman's face. Blood sprayed across the ground. He shook his hand to ease the pain in his knuckles.

"One night, when I was lying in the arms of a soiled dove named Margaret, I had an epiphany! Now I know it's my fate to liberate the west. I am the lord of these territories. I am the king of outlaws," Ivan continued. "I will restore things to the way they were in the good old days, the times when outlaws ruled. And you have impeded my progress one time too many."

"You've terrorized the folks of this great state for nine years," the Texas Ranger hissed. "Someone is goin' to put a stop to it. If it ain't me, then it'll be someone else."

Ivan held his hand out and waited for Victor to place a pistol in his hand. The comforting weight of the gun was like an embrace from an old friend after years of separation. He tapped the Texas Ranger's forehead with the gun and watched the man flinch. "I'm going to kill two people today, Ranger, and I'm going to let you choose which one of you is going to live to tell the tale."

"You're a twisted man…"

He squatted down in front of the lawmen and shoved the pistol beneath the Texas Ranger's chin. "I don't take kindly to insults." Ivan sneered between tightly clenched teeth. "But congratulations, Ranger, you answered my request without having to sully your reputation. I have kept you alive." The flash of fear in his enemy's eyes was nearly as satisfying as the startled cry of the deputy beside him. Ivan stood up, straightened to his full height, and moved to stand behind the lawmen. There was no hesitation in his actions nor regret in his cold, black heart as he pulled the trigger.

The first deputy fell facedown in the dirt.

"All right!" shouted the Texas Ranger. "You've proven your point! I learned my lesson. I won't come after you… Just let us go, and you can walk away right now."

Ivan tossed his head back and cackled like a madman. He pulled the trigger once more, and the second deputy toppled over. Victor handed Ivan a handkerchief. The outlaw wiped away the blood from his face as he replied, "Killing you would be too easy. I want you to suffer, to live out your days knowing these men died because you got in my way."

Chapter 2

Gaptooth Canyon, Texas

Shadows crept across the land as the sun dipped behind the canyon wall. Tracker and Abe sat huddled around their fire in the valley below, both scraping away at the last bite of beans at the bottom of their dented cans. Work was slow the further east they traveled, but the bounty hunters enjoyed the rare night off. Getting lost in the wilds with a friend and a good horse was the ideal life for a man like Abe.

The sound of fish jumping in the quarry lake just a few feet from their camp mingled with the crackling fire. Tracker tossed his empty bean can beside the hole they had dug for food scraps and reclined against his bedroll. "We could stay here," he said in a deep, rumbling voice. "There's enough land to build a ranch."

"Thinking about retiring?" Abe asked.

"Perhaps."

"I guess with the clay deposits, fresh water source, and the grasslands just a few miles up the valley, it would make sense," he mused. "Sheep or cattle could thrive here. Maybe even horses."

Tracker pulled out his knife with a shrug and whittled away at a piece of wood he had carried with him for weeks. "It would be a good place for you to start a family and—"

Abe lifted his hand to cut off Tracker's words. "I'm not interested in any of that right now," he sighed. "Besides, I'm too busy keeping you out of trouble. I've already retired my father's guns. No need to rush into any more changes."

An owl let out a hoot from its perch along the ridge as the pounding of approaching hooves echoed through the valley. Abe and Tracker lifted their weapons and aimed them toward the path that led to their camp. Tracker's bowstring was pulled tight with an arrow notched and ready to soar.

Abe's finger ghosted over the trigger of his firearm. "Show yourself," he ordered their uninvited guest. "Keep your hands where I can see them."

The rider pulled back on the reins, slowing his horse before he hopped down from the saddle. Light from the campfire glimmered off a badge pinned to the man's shirt. "My name is Hunter Greene," the man said as he approached them wearily with his arms hanging loose by his sides. "I'm a Texas Ranger."

"What brings you to our camp, Ranger?" Abe shifted closer, but he kept his gun raised to Ranger Greene's chest.

"I heard there were bounty hunters seen passin' through Rodeo Springs a few weeks back, and I thought I should see why they were in the region," the ranger replied. "You wouldn't know anythin' about it, would you?"

Tracker lowered his bow before Abe could answer. He set his weapon near his bedroll and walked up to the Texas Ranger. "My name is Tracker, and this my partner Abraham Delaney."

Recognition flashed in Ranger Greene's eyes the moment Tracker uttered Abe's name. Abe couldn't help the curse that fell from his lips. All he wanted was some peace and quiet after all they had been through in the last year or so, but it didn't seem like he was getting what he wanted anytime soon. Especially not when the look of recognition was followed by an expression of relief. "You have no idea how glad I am to have found you, Mr. Delaney," Greene said. "I've been lookin' for you since the rumors of your arrival in Texas first started."

"We try not to make ourselves too easy to find," Tracker snorted. "There are days when friends and enemies share the same face."

Ranger Greene dug around in his pocket and pulled out a scrap of paper that was all too familiar to Abe: it was a contract. The bounty hunter returned his sidearm to its holster and held his hand out. Greene dropped the contract into Abe's palm before he turned to shake Tracker's hand.

"You're after an outlaw called the Reaper?" Abe asked as he read over the paper.

Greene scratched at his jaw and nodded. "Ivan 'the Reaper' Lincoln has friends in high and low places. His capture needs to be done quietly and without a body count longer than the Mississippi."

"Why so cautious?" Tracker questioned.

Abe held the contract out for his partner to see. He pointed to the bottom half of the page labeled as a confidentiality clause. "Because Ivan Lincoln is the son of the San Antonio mayor," he revealed to Tracker. "And I reckon that upcoming election would swing in the opponent's favor if word got out the mayor's son is an outlaw."

"Not just any outlaw," Ranger Greene muttered. "He's known as the king of outlaws. I've tried to arrest him over a dozen times in the past nine years and he has escaped every attempt unscathed and with a pile of dead lawmen in his wake."

"What's he after?"

"Ivan was raised back east with his mother, but he places no value on civilized life," the ranger explained to Abe. "He claims he wants to liberate the west and return it to the times when outlaws were runnin' things. Says his father's work is a failure because the mayor wants to build a prison a few miles outside of the city so outlaws like Ivan get locked away for good."

Abe nodded his head, along with the ranger's words. He believed the punishment an outlaw received at the end of their trial should have measured up to the crime, that murderers deserve to be hanged for what they did, but he knew there were folks who disagreed. "The bounty says he's wanted for murder and arson," Abe said. "But what is it you aren't telling us?"

"The mayor didn't want me to tell you the reason they call him the Reaper..."

***

San Antonio, Texas

Tracker didn't like the situation one bit.

He stood beside the bookshelf in the mayor's office, glancing up at the framed photographs on the wall—none of which featured the man's son. But after what Ranger Greene had told them about the Reaper, it did not surprise Tracker there was bad blood between the mayor and Ivan Lincoln. Apparently, Tracker and Abraham's target had a nasty habit of killing any lawman or bounty hunter that spoke his name out loud, appearing as if out of thin air to do away with anyone who tried to take him down.

All outlaws wanted their own legend, and the Reaper had so far proven his to be true.

Outlaws were something he could deal with. It was the mayor that made Tracker uncomfortable. Politicians were some of the slimiest people he had ever crossed paths with while on the road with Abraham. They were the sort that hired outlaws to do their dirty work, all while smiling in the public's face, giving speeches in the town hall about cracking down on crime. It was the dishonesty and lack of remorse that made his skin crawl.

Tracker knew his partner felt the same about politicians, which made him curious why Abraham had agreed to meet with the mayor in secret. His gaze flickered over to the window where Ranger Greene pulled the curtains closed and blocked out the view of San Antonio, washed in the shadows of the late night. The lawman had been right to tell us about the Reaper, but Tracker could see it had broken something inside of him to do so. He wasn't sure what the mayor had done to earn Ranger Greene's loyalty. Abraham must have been on a similar train of thought because he asked, "Why is a Texas Ranger like yourself acting like a hired nanny for the mayor's son?"

Ranger Greene scrubbed a hand over his face and leaned against the large oak desk at the center of the room. "I owe him."

Tracker met his partner's gaze as they shared a skeptical look before Abraham prodded further. "And why is that?"

"It's personal."

"If it could get in the way of us capturing the Reaper, we must know," Tracker replied. He watched the lawman closely, noting how he hesitated when answering a simple question. While Tracker admired the loyalty the ranger had for the mayor, it also made him suspicious.

Finally, after nearly an hour of waiting, the mayor arrived. Henry Jameson was unlike the politicians and town officials Tracker had met in the past. The man was so tall he had to duck his head just to walk through his office door. He had wide shoulders and quite a bit of muscle, despite the weathered appearance of his skin and the gray threading through his hair. Tracker realized Mayor Jameson wasn't the sort of man who shied away from a hard day's labor.

"I must apologize for all the secrecy, but we're all on edge with the election coming up," the mayor chuckled as he held out a calloused hand for Abraham to shake. Tracker watched the cordial exchange between them, looking for any sign of... well, Tracker wasn't sure, but something about the whole situation stank of treachery.

"Pleasure to meet you, Mr. Mayor," Abraham replied politely. "Forgive us if we seem a little apprehensive. It's just that we find it difficult to believe an outlaw with a gang as small as the Reaper's has avoided the gallows this long."

"My son is a very intelligent person, but he's unpredictable." Mayor Jameson rounded the corner of his desk and took a seat in the chair. "Ivan thinks ten steps ahead of us, and he's far more willing to endanger the lives of others to get what he wants."

"What caused the two of you to fall out?" Abraham asked.

Tracker moved closer to his partner and met the mayor's gaze, silently urging the man to be honest with Abraham. He was not ignorant to the fact his presence intimidated most people, his Comanche blood making many nervous.

Mayor Jameson proved he was no different. He swallowed noisily and fumbled with the papers on his desk before he answered. "I must admit I was not always the best father when Ivan was younger. I chose my career over my family, and it pushed my wife away. She took Ivan and moved east with her parents."

"He resented you for it."

"Yes," the mayor sighed. "When Ivan returned to Texas, he made it known he wanted nothing to do with the legacy that I worked so hard to build for him. He said he was going to make his own legacy… one that spat in the face of everything I believed in."

Tracker snorted. "A success, I would say."

The hurt in the mayor's gaze was unmistakable. "Ivan might have chosen a different path than I had in mind for him, but he's still my son. I love him dearly, and it causes me a great deal of pain to see the suffering he has caused others because I was a fool."

Abraham shook his head and leaned over the desk. "With all due respect, Mr. Mayor, this ain't a boy rustling up a commotion because his daddy took away his favorite toy. This is an outlaw with a vendetta. You best start seeing the difference, or else you might not like how this ends. Do I make myself clear?"

To Tracker's surprise, the mayor didn't back down. Mayor Jameson tapped his fingers against the top of the desk and replied, "I understand what you're saying, Mr. Delaney, but let me make myself clear. If you kill my son, I won't pay you a single dime. The contract you signed before coming here has a clause stating I did not sanction the killing of Ivan "the Reaper" Lincoln. His death means the end of your bounty hunting career and the start of your days as a wanted man. So you best start seeing the difference."

There it was, Tracker realized as his stomach dropped. There was the catch he had feared all along.

He glared over at Abraham and saw the tension in his partner's shoulders. Anger radiated off him like an aura. Tracker placed his hand on Abraham's arm and pulled him back from the desk before he did something stupid. From the looks of things, Ranger Greene hadn't been aware of the clause within the contract either. The lawman clenched his jaw so hard that Tracker heard his teeth grind.

"He's responsible for over three dozen—"

"I know!" shouted the mayor, cutting off Ranger Greene's angry words. "I am well aware of the charges against my son. But I also know Mr. Delaney has showed outlaws mercy, to give them a chance at a fair trial."

Abraham shook his head in what appeared to be disbelief. "You don't know me, Mr. Mayor. My reputation and the rumors of my mercy do not define who I am. The fact of the matter is I will kill any outlaw that leaves me no choice."

"If you won't do it for yourself or your reputation, then do it for your partner," Mayor Jameson suggested. "The law won't be kind to a Comanche accused of murder."

Shocked by the mayor's threats, Tracker hadn't been quick enough to grab his partner before Abraham leaped across the desk. The sound of snapping bone and a loud thud rang through the office.

Chapter 3

Abe heard the keys to the jail cell jingle as he cracked open his eyes the following morning. The pain in his knuckles throbbed something fierce, and he had a headache brewing behind his right eye. Ranger Greene might be a naïve man with unshakeable loyalty, but he had one hell of a right hook. Abe supposed he deserved a punch to the face after he attacked the mayor, but in his defense, folks targeting Tracker with unwarranted bigotry had always been a sore spot for him.

"Mr. Delaney," a sweet voice called from just beyond the iron bars of his cell.

"Yeah..."

"You look terrible," the woman cackled. "What did you do to get thrown in here?"

"I... uh... hit someone."

A humorous snort echoed in the cell as she fumbled with the keys. "Well, seeing as the mayor is wearing several bruises of the same color," she began, "I'd say the two of you had a slight disagreement."

Abe pushed himself up into a sitting position, fighting back the nausea that burned in the back of his throat. His swollen, bloodshot eyes landed on a petite woman wearing a hat that was far too big for her head and a double-breasted waistcoat over her blouse. While women were less likely to work as hired guns, it wasn't impossible, so Abe wasn't too surprised by the novelty of her status. However, he found it hard to imagine a pretty little thing like her, with a mop of auburn curls on her head and freckles on her nose, as a gunslinger, despite the pistols strapped to her hips.

He stood slowly and approached the bars, careful not to get too close as she blinked her big blue eyes up at him. "Morning," he drawled around a yawn that stretched his mouth wide open. "You are?"

"Lucy," she stated matter-of-factly. "But you can call me Miss Baker."

"So no husband to approve of you working as a mercenary, ma'am?" Abe asked with a wolfish grin.

"If my husband were alive, I'm sure he would understand the men of this city are too afraid to do something about the outlaws." Lucy tucked a stray curl behind her ear and unlocked the cell.

Abe's smile faltered. He cleared his throat and ran a hand through his messy hair. "Please excuse my ignorance, ma'am. I'm sorry for your loss."

"I ain't," she said with a shrug. "Only knew him for about a week, but it was long enough to know John got what he deserved."

Abe wasn't sure how to respond, so he grabbed his hat from the hook near the door and plopped it onto his head. "You said the men were too afraid to handle the outlaws. Why aren't you?"

Lucy shrugged once more. She hopped up onto the chair behind the sheriff's desk and propped her feet up. "I lived a hard life in South Carolina, and I ain't afraid of hard work. The only way I could escape my past was to get married. I found an advertisement in the paper for a man looking for a wife, and I got on the first train to Texas after he responded to my letter," she explained. "John and I married before I found out he was wanted for hurting women. So I suppose I'm just so used to being scared that I hardly notice danger anymore. Working for the mayor to make sure you don't break your contract seemed as good a job as any."

"You're a brave woman."

She tossed her head back and laughed at the notion. "Brave? Brave is pummeling the mayor. You're the brave one, Mr. Delaney. I married a madman. Some would say that makes me a glutton for trouble."

"I don't know about that," he replied. Abe smiled at Lucy's honesty. It was a refreshing change after meeting the mayor. In fact, genuine people were about as rare to find as gold over the past year.

"Oh?" she snickered. "Are you a glutton for trouble too?"

He leaned against the desk and gingerly touched his swollen eye. "I don't go looking for it, no, but it seems trouble likes to follow me everywhere I go despite my good intentions."

Mischief glittered in Lucy's eyes as her lopsided grin widened. "You know what they say about misery loving company..."

***

The Kingdom

15 miles from San Antonio, Texas

A loud ruckus blared through the open windows of the king's house. Ivan sat upon a makeshift throne fashioned from ammunition crates as he picked a chunk of salted meat from between his teeth. The gang cheered on as Victor and Angus arm wrestled at a nearby table. Drinks sloshed over the rims of cups, sticky globs of mashed potatoes fell onto the wobbling table, and chairs scraped against the floor as Ivan looked on at the unadulterated shenanigans that took place in his home. Such behavior was frowned upon by his mother's sort, which made him enjoy it all the more.

The door swung open.

A gust of stale summer wind fluttered inside, causing the lanterns to flicker. Ivan peered over at the door as one of his scouts entered the room. The hefty outlaw lumbered over to the throne and whispered into Ivan's ear, "There's a house just a ways down the river. Folks say the farmer and his young daughter got silver."

Ivan scratched at his jaw with a frown. "How many people are on the farm besides the owner and his daughter?"

"Three. A stable boy and two maids."

"No security?" he asked with a huff. "They're practically begging for us to relieve them of their treasures." Ivan stood up with a groan. He pressed a hand to his tender ribs and whistled to get his men's attention. "Saddle up."

The gang jumped to action, tossing back their drinks before they stumbled toward the door with a slew of curses on their lips. Victor moved to Ivan's side and stayed there until the horses were ready. "Where are we headed?" Victor asked his boss. "I thought the plan was to lie low for a few months."

Ivan headed out toward the stables. "This one seems too good to pass up," he said. "Besides, I'm growing bored with this sneaking around."

They climbed into their saddles and rode along the riverbank. It wasn't long before Ivan spotted flickering lights through the windows of the farmhouse. He pulled back on the reins with a soft, "Whoa, boy."

The horse stopped just shy of the fence that surrounded the farm. Ivan gestured with his hand, and three men circled around toward the back. He slid down from his perch and hitched his mount to the fence. Victor and two outlaws in the gang followed his lead. They crept closer to the farmhouse with their guns drawn and their eyes peeled for any sign of trouble. Victor and Ivan flanked the front door. Jerry crouched down between them and slid a lock pick from his back pocket. The outlaw fiddled with the lock on the door as Ivan peered in through the window.

Jerry turned the lock pick, and the door swung open gently. Victor let the others in through the back door while Ivan inched his way toward the staircase. One by one, they doused the lanterns, bathing the rooms in darkness, and the gang pillaged the farmer's house.

Ivan stepped lightly as he ascended the stairs. His boots scuffed on the weathered boards that gave a slight groan beneath his weight. He reached the landing on the second floor and slithered along the wall as if he were one with the shadows.

Suddenly, a crash came from the kitchen.

The bedchamber door flew open and banged against the wall. Ivan held his breath and waited until the farmer stepped out into the hallway to investigate the noise. When the barrel of a shotgun came into his line of sight, Ivan counted down the seconds before the man came around the corner. He reared his arm back and struck hard and fast, bashing his gun into the back of the farmer's head until he crumpled to the floor. The second bedchamber door opened, and the farmer's daughter let out a shrill cry at the sight of her father's unconscious form.

Ivan grabbed the girl and slammed her against the wall, cutting her scream off as the air rushed from her lungs. She swung her fists and tried to fight him off, but he wrapped his hand around her throat and gave a little squeeze. The effect was almost instant. Fear flashed in her eyes. The woman's arms dropped to her sides. Ivan felt her throat work against the palm of his hand as she swallowed nervously.

Footfalls came from the staircase, and then Victor stood beside Ivan.

"What should we do with her?" the gang leader asked, with a ruthless smile curling on his lips. "Should we kill her?"

The woman let out a whimper.

Victor shook his head. "I say we bring her along and put her to work. We could use someone around who can cook and clean."

Ivan stepped away from the girl and clapped his hands loudly. "I like that," he exclaimed. "No use in wasting such a pretty sight, either. Bind her hands and toss her over your horse. We'll take the stable boy too."

As Victor rushed to do as he was told, Ivan called downstairs for his men to search the second floor as well. They ransacked the entire farmhouse, leaving no stone unturned. Ivan moved toward the small room near the kitchens and found the maids huddled together in the corner. Tears streamed from their eyes as they prayed out loud.

His face was an emotionless mask of indifference when he lifted his gun, squeezed the trigger twice, and delivered them to their savior.

Jerry came up behind Ivan and said, "That's cold, boss."

Ivan chuckled as he reached into his pocket and pulled out a handkerchief. "Wouldn't do us much good if we left witnesses. It's best if we keep the law off our backs for now," he replied. "What did the boys find?"

"There's some family heirlooms and trinkets we found. I reckon we could fence them for a decent profit."

"Good," Ivan said. "Check the barn, grab any livestock and sell them to the nearby ranches while you're at it."

"What are you going to do?"

Ivan didn't answer Jerry.

He simply walked into the kitchen and looted around in the cupboards until he found a few bottles of liquor. The dastardly gang leader poured the contents of the bottles all over the floor of the kitchen and sitting room before he struck a sulfur on the wall. He laughed and laughed as he flicked the match onto the soaked ground, watching as the flames crawled across the floorboards.

Chapter 4

San Antonio, Texas

While Abraham asked around town about the Reaper, Tracker contacted a man who owed him a great debt. He met with Jeremiah Wilson at the hotel near the saloon. Jeremiah was a solicitor who wasn't afraid to bend the rules—in fact, Tracker supposed, Jeremiah broke them more often than not. Oddly enough, it was the very reason he had asked to meet with Jeremiah.

Tracker knocked on the door and waited patiently for it to open. Jeremiah wore a smile that was strained around the edges, a practiced smile that had swindled far too many folks out of their livelihoods for Tracker's comfort. "My, my, if it ain't my old friend Tracker," Jeremiah chuckled. "How long has it been?"

"Three years."

"Time sure flies." The crooked solicitor gestured to the chair in the room's corner, and Tracker humored him by taking a seat. Jeremiah Wilson didn't have friends. He had a list of people who owed him and a list of people he owed. Tracker was glad to be part of the latter group.

He reached into his pocket, pulled out his copy of the mayor's contract, and handed it to Jeremiah. "I need to know if this clause about Ivan Lincoln is real."

Jeremiah took a pair of spectacles from the bedside table and slid them up the bridge of his nose as he peered down at the paper in his hands. "It's a legitimate document, that's for sure," the solicitor muttered. "It states clearly that if Ivan Lincoln is killed in your custody that you will be punished within the full extent of the law and charged with murder."

"He's a killer."

"And a darn good one," Jeremiah snorted. "Ivan Lincoln has a place near to here called the Kingdom. It ain't nothing more than an old mining town, but he's determined to make something out of it. Folks say you can hear screams all the way down the road coming from that place."

Tracker stood up and slammed his fist against the wall. "So you're saying we have no choice but to bring him in alive?"

To his credit, Jeremiah barely batted an eyelash at Tracker's uncharacteristic loss of control. "If you so much as harm a single hair on Ivan Lincoln's head, you'll end up in a cell just like the one you were in when you met Abraham Delaney."

Tracker shook the dust from his hand. And wiggled his fingers to make sure none of them had broken. "We only have seven weeks to find and arrest a man they claim cannot be captured," Tracker complained. "We have no badges and—"

"And you cannot use the mayor's name as leverage in your investigation," Jeremiah interrupted. "What about Ranger Greene?"

"He is too loyal to the mayor."

"Then you better find someone willing to help you who knows a bit about Lincoln, or I'm afraid you're out of luck." The solicitor sat on the edge of his bed and removed the spectacles. "In the meantime, I'll take a better look at this contract to make sure there ain't any loopholes."

"Thank you."

"It's the least I can do for the man who saved my life," Jeremiah said with a smile that seemed far more genuine than the one he usually wore.

Tracker shook Jeremiah's hand and left before the sun set. He made his way across town and found the inn near the post office where they had rented a room. Tracker avoided the front of the building and tiptoed in through the back to not draw any unwanted attention. He hurried through the corridor and unlocked their room.

Abraham and a woman Tracker didn't recognize stood beside the window. He cleared his throat to get his partner's attention. But when Abraham met Tracker's stare, there was something different in his pale blue eyes. It was a look Tracker had never seen on Abraham before. There was a spark of joy that seemed so out of place for the stoic bounty hunter.

"Miss Baker, this here is my partner, Tracker," Abraham announced. "Tracker, this is Lucy Baker. She's a hired gun that works as an enforcer for the mayor."

"Why would the mayor need a hired gun?" Tracker asked.

"Pleasure to meet you," the woman said as she ignored his question.

"And you," he replied before turning to his partner once more. "Why is she in our room?"

"She agreed to help us with Ivan Lincoln."

Tracker took a step back and shut the door quietly. "Did you forget our target has a talent for killing?" he snapped. "You are putting her life in danger—"

"Whoa, whoa!" Abraham waved his hands wildly. "What's gotten into you? I've never seen you this shaken up before."

Tracker hung his head before he replied, "The mayor could ruin me with a snap of his fingers, Abraham. Although the wars between my people and the settlers are over, the tribes are still trying to fight. You will get a trial if this goes badly, so our situations are not the same. If I don't end up imprisoned, they will hang me."

Abraham rested his hand on Tracker's shoulder and met his stare with unwavering determination. "You're my partner and my brother, Tracker. I would watch the world burn before I let that happen." The dark promise lingered in the room, hovering between them. Tracker knew his partner was a man of his word. He clapped Abraham on the arm and pulled him in for a brotherly hug.

Abe released Tracker before he turned around to face Lucy. The young mercenary had a smile on her face that made him nervous. It wasn't often he allowed anyone close enough to gauge just how much he respected his partner. Abe felt shaken by Lucy. He couldn't quite seem to keep his guard up around her, and it made him uncomfortable.

She plopped down in the chair near the beds and removed the oversized hat from her head. "I don't trust the mayor as far as I can throw him," Lucy sighed. "But I trust Ranger Greene. He's an honorable man when he ain't blinded by the mayor's pretty words. You boys will need a plan if we're going after the Reaper."

"You are not going after the Reaper," Abe shot back. "Tracker and I are going after him while you keep an eye on the town."

"Hogwash!"

Abe lifted his brow and met her challenge head-on. Lucy was a powerful woman, but he wasn't the sort of man to put a woman's life in danger if he could help it. "I'm not arguing with you, Miss Baker. Either you stay here and keep an eye on things, or you don't get to help at all."

Lucy jumped up out of her chair, placing herself only inches away from Abe. She poked him in the chest and sneered. "You don't tell me what to do, Abraham Delaney! The only way you'll be able to make heads or tails of all this is if I'm with you."

Tracker bit his lip to keep from laughing, and Abe shot him a deadly glare.

"Listen here, woman," the bounty hunter shouted. "I won't be responsible for you getting killed. We have enough to deal with without having to worry about you getting shot or kidnapped. The odds of us walking away from this fight are slim."

Lucy didn't back down. She crossed her arms over her chest and smiled. There was a stubborn look in her blue eyes that made Abe want to break something. "I wager twenty dollars I can shoot better than you with my eyes shut," she chuckled. "Another twenty if I can plant you on your hind end in a fight."

"This isn't a game…"

"Why not?" Lucy asked. "We know the Reaper for playing games, Mr. Delaney. You ride in there without me, and you may as well have the undertaker dig your grave right now."

Tracker seemed to take an interest in her words. Abe watched as his partner approached Lucy. To her credit, there was no immediate reaction in her expression. "Why would the Reaper allow you into his camp?" Tracker asked, as he watched her.

Lucy glanced over at Abe and pulled the sleeve of her blouse up to her elbow. A long scar was revealed. It was dark and jagged, slashing through the pale complexion of her skin. "Because he saved me from my husband," she revealed. "Ivan Lincoln is a cruel man, there's no doubt about that, but things ain't as black and white as the mayor would have you believe."

Abe looked away, trying to stamp down the fury that boiled in his veins at the thought of anyone hurting Lucy.

"I had gone to the sheriff many times after my husband's anger got out of control," she continued. "No one did anything about it. The men in this city were a bunch of lazy drunkards."

"And Ivan took it upon himself to step in?" Abe asked.

Lucy shook her head. "I went to Mr. Jameson for help before he became mayor. He always said he respected women, so I thought he might help me. The day John gave me this scar was the last time I saw him alive. It was Jameson who sent Ivan to kill my husband."

Abe tensed. He took a deep breath and then reached out for Lucy. She stepped closer as he placed his hands on her arm. "Are you saying that Mayor Jameson ordered his son to execute your husband?"

When Lucy nodded slowly, Abe thought the world had stopped spinning for several heartbeats. "Ivan told his father that John had been taken care of, and the next morning, he was a wanted man," she informed them. "Jameson used Ivan to start his career as mayor and then tossed him to the wolves. That's why he became an outlaw."

Abe backed away from Lucy and wandered over to the window. He threw open the shutters to let in some of the cool night breeze to dry the sweat that clung to his brow. If what Lucy said was true, their job just got a lot more complicated.

"There's only seven weeks until the election. That's seven weeks to bring Ivan Lincoln to justice," he growled as his fingers curled tightly over the windowsill.

Lucy shuffled across the room, once again placing herself in Abe's space. "They hired me to watch you, and I intend to do so, but not because of Jameson. Let's go look at his camp, and then we can decide, but I think he'll talk to me."

"We should at least try," Tracker added. "She might convince him to come along peacefully."

Abe still wasn't convinced they weren't offering her up like a sacrifice. He slammed the window shut and nodded his head. "All right, but the second I sense the meeting going sour, I'm pulling you out of there," he said to Lucy. "Ranger

Greene thinks Ivan has become unstable after their last run-in, so he might not remember you."

"He will." Lucy placed her hand on her hip, sounding so sure that Abe almost believed her. But like most people, Lucy had a tell. Abe smiled knowingly as she tucked an auburn curl behind her ear.

He bent forward to bring his face a little closer to hers, watching the rosy blush creep across her cheeks. "Then why do I get the impression, the only one in this room afraid of Ivan is you," Abe whispered accusingly. "The story of your husband was clever, Mrs. Lincoln, but I don't believe a single word of it."

Chapter 5

Tracker leaned against the rock wall facing the old mining town the Reaper turned into his personal kingdom. Only a handful of armed outlaws roamed the sidewalks. The rest of the people appeared to be servants in one form or another. But the iron collars around their necks made Tracker think they were more hostages than paid employees.

A rustle to his left signaled Miss Baker's approach.

"See anything?"

Tracker remained silent, unwilling to reveal anything to a woman who lied as easily as she breathed.

Miss Baker took his silence as an invitation to explain herself. "Look, I get you ain't likely to trust me anytime soon," she huffed as she leaned against the wall beside him. "But I wanted you to know the truth."

Tracker shifted away from her and crouched down to pick up his bow.

"I really came to Texas to get married," Miss Baker claimed. "But I was supposed to marry Ivan Lincoln. Jameson was a cattle baron back then, and he wanted grandchildren, someone to give the ranch to when he died. Things didn't work out the way he planned."

Tracker continued to work in the quiet as the sun rose. He pretended not to listen, but he couldn't deny her story could have something of value to use against the Reaper if necessary.

"Ivan was a kind man," she continued. "He knew I didn't love him, but he tried his best to keep me happy. It was his father who was the problem. Jameson made Ivan do bad things, and when I found out he had killed someone for his father, I got upset and tried to leave him."

A small hand rested upon his shoulder, causing Tracker to nearly drop his precious bow over the ridge.

Miss Baker crouched beside him and forced him to look her in the eyes as she said, "I got an annulment on my marriage with Ivan, and I think... I think the disappointment made Jameson see him as nothing more than a puppet on a string. Someone he could toss aside when he finally got what he wanted."

"Why are you telling me this?" Tracker finally asked.

"Because I feel as though I've broken your trust before I even earned it," Miss Baker replied. "And I know the only way to get Mr. Delaney to trust me—"

"You like him?"

Her face turned a bright hue of crimson as she nibbled on her bottom lip coyly. "I do, yes," she stammered. "But we've only just met, and I've already lied so much."

"To protect yourself?"

Miss Baker shook her head. "To protect Ivan," she corrected. "I can handle anything, but Ivan has always been fragile. I suppose I wanted someone to see he wasn't a cruel man when I met him. He was a victim at first, only guilty of trying to impress a father he barely knew."

Tracker gently removed her hand from his shoulder and stood up. "The Reaper must take responsibility for his actions," he stated. "It doesn't matter who he was when you married him. All that matters is he became the monster his father nurtured. He had choices, and he chose wrong."

"How many people have you killed?"

"Too many to count and none of them innocent."

"Who gave you the right to decide their innocence?" she shouted. "Who are you to judge their actions if your own aren't saintly?"

"I kill murderers, thieves, and men who would make you pray to your god for death if they ever got their hands on you," Tracker explained. "I kill only when I have to and never without a good reason."

Miss Baker adjusted her hat nervously, annoying Tracker for the last time.

Tracker sighed and snatched it from her head. She attempted to take it back until he handed her the one lying beside his bedroll, the one that used to belong to Abraham. It was much smaller than the floppy hat she constantly fiddled with.

"Thank you."

"Abraham needs to protect you," Tracker said suddenly. "He needs to protect everyone. Show him you can be trusted, that you don't need his protection, and he will see you as his equal."

"I thought you would... I don't know... tell me to leave him be," she laughed softly. "Does this mean I've redeemed myself?"

"It means I will not stop you from proving you can be more than just a beautiful woman who lies to get what she wants," he replied with a brutal serving of honesty. Tracker packed up his things and headed back toward their small camp.

Abraham stirred when he sensed them drawing closer. He cracked open his sleep-deprived eyes as Tracker tossed him a can of biscuits.

"No meat?" Abe grumbled.

"No. Hunting would be too risky when we are camped so close to the Kingdom," he replied. The heat rose with the morning light. Tracker peeled off his jacket and laid it across his lap. Even his vest seemed much too hot.

Abraham kicked off his blanket with an irritable groan before he glanced between Tracker and Miss Baker. "What happened while I was trying to sleep?"

"A truce of sorts," Miss Baker provided.

Abraham seemed a little suspicious of the idea, but he bit his tongue. Tracker sat back and watched his partner interact with their temporary ally. He couldn't deny there was a spark of attraction between them, even if it made him uneasy. His partner deserved to have a normal life, a family of his own, and a home to retire to. Tracker wasn't convinced a woman as complicated as Lucy Baker was the right woman for Abraham.

***

San Antonio, Texas

Waves of heat rippled up from the ground. Abe wiped his arm across his forehead and adjusted the brim of his hat. Steel-blue eyes scanned the valley below, observing how the outlaws moved from one decrepit building to the next. It still wasn't clear what Ivan Lincoln had planned for the old mining town. In fact, there was very little information about the outlaw that Abe trusted.

Miss Lucy Baker, Ranger Greene, and Mayor Jameson had lied about Ivan's motives since the beginning. If Abe and Tracker had any hope of capturing their target, they needed to learn the truth. Sadly, the only way for them to know Ivan "the Reaper" Lincoln's motives was to talk to the man himself, which was something Abe thought might be easier than convincing Tracker it was a good idea.

Tracker had a sixth sense for telling when Abe had a bad idea. He lowered the binoculars and looked over at Abe. "What is it?"

"Nothing."

"You've gone quiet," Tracker pointed out. "And that usually means you have a plan."

Abe snorted and shook his head. "You ain't going to like what I have to say."

"Say it anyway."

He moved to sit beside his partner as he wiped the sweat from his eyes. Their long legs dangled over the edge of the steep drop that hovered above the valley. "We need to meet with Ivan," Abe suggested. "Right now, I don't know who we're hunting, and I don't like feeling like I'm walking into a fight blind."

Tracker toyed with the end of his braided hair, refusing to look Abe in the eyes as he said, "We can't just walk in there."

"Actually, I think we can." Abe leaned toward his partner and lowered his voice to a whisper. "These men do not know who we are. I say we dress up like bandits and pretend like we're holding Lucy hostage. If Ivan still cares about her the way she thinks he does, then he'll agree to talk. Get him alone and then take him down."

"It's risky," Tracker hissed. "They could shoot us at the gates before we even lay eyes on the Reaper. I've been watching them. He's unstable. Twitchy and talking to himself when he thinks no one is looking."

"Do you have a better plan?" Abe rubbed at the back of his neck to relieve the knots that formed beneath the skin from all the stress.

"She could turn on us, Abraham," his partner said softly.

Abe opened his eyes and looked over at Tracker with a frown. "You think she's working with Ivan Lincoln? After everything she's told you about him?"

"We do not know if any of it is true," Tracker sighed. "Ranger Greene doesn't know how the Reaper has predicted their plans to capture him. Lucy Baker has lied to us to protect a man she claims she wants to put behind bars, but I do not think it is unreasonable to believe she would become a hired gun to keep that from happening."

"So Lucy is some sort of master of manipulation? Feeding Ivan information from the inside? That's a ridiculous notion, even for your suspicious mind."

Tracker shrugged. "She got you to agree to let her come with us. I can't shake the feeling we are delivering her to her former husband."

"No," Abe said. He scooted back from the ledge and stood up, brushing his pants off. "I refuse to believe all of this is some ploy to reunite with Ivan. She could have manipulated Ranger Greene or any other fool in San Antonio, but she didn't. She's here with us now because she wants Ivan put away."

"Then why lie to us? Why not tell us the truth from the beginning?"

"Maybe she was afraid we would judge her," he answered. "How many people sneered at her when they found out she used to be married to Ivan? I can imagine she has lived a troubled life, just like you and I, and she's learned not to trust others just on principle alone."

Their conversation ended when Lucy rode up on her horse. The mangy old bag of fleas huffed and puffed, swishing his tail as flies buzzed all around. Abe curled his lip in distaste and wondered why she couldn't have purchased something that wasn't wind-broken and smelled like it was an inch from death. It said a lot about who she was as a person. It was proof she saw value in things most people would have turned their backs on.

Like Ivan Lincoln.

"What did you find?" Abe called out to Lucy.

"There's a farmhouse up the river that was nearly burned to bits." She crouched beside the camp and picked up the water canteen before taking a big swig. "I could look inside. Part of me wishes I hadn't."

"Bodies?"

"Yep," Lucy replied, visibly shaken by whatever horrors she had stumbled upon. "Three from what I saw, but there were a lot of tracks leading away from wreckage."

"Tracker, I want you to check it out," Abe requested. "Miss Baker and I will pack up the camp and discuss the plan for tonight. Be careful."

Tracker tilted his head toward Abe before he went to fetch his horse.

Abe patted Lucy's mount as his partner rode off down the path. "You've been watching Ivan for a long time," he started. "What do you know about the men in his gang?"

"There's five men in his gang. Victor, Jerry, Angus, Jasper, and Wade. Victor is his right-hand man," Lucy explained. "He's just as vile and ruthless as Ivan."

"And the others?"

"They follow Ivan for the pay, not out of loyalty." She ran her fingers through the horse's mane, leaning against his side as she glanced up at Abe.

He swallowed past the lump in his throat. The hole in his chest where his heart was supposed to be seemed less empty when he looked at her. Abe knew she had lied to protect Ivan, but his instincts were screaming for him to trust her. "We want to put on a bit of a performance," he said around a tongue that felt much too thick. No woman had ever affected him like Lucy has. "Tracker and I will dress like bandits and take you into the Kingdom as a hostage. We'll demand to speak with Ivan alone and then make our move."

Lucy chewed on her bottom lip and looked as if she were in deep thought. "You want us to bluff our way in and hope Ivan don't shoot you?"

"I know it's a risk, but I would rather you have Tracker and I as backup than to have you go in there on your own," he muttered irritably. "Ivan might not be the same man you remember."

Lucy's shoulders slumped forward as she stepped away from her mount. "I know… but I need to see for myself there's no hope of him changing. I might not love Ivan, but I feel as if I was the one who caused this."

"He made his choice."

"Your partner said the same thing," she scoffed.

"And he's right."

Lucy's heavy-lidded expression made Abe shift on his heels a little. "The mayor thinks I'm better at breaking a man than I am at slinging a pistol. He sees me as some heartless wench who ruined his son. Maybe that's the real reason he sent me here," she said. "Maybe he wanted me to break you too."

Abe cocked his head to the side and felt himself move closer to Lucy. The scent of lilac and clean sweat reached his nose, mingling in a heady concoction. "Is that so? Do you think you can break a man like me, Miss Baker?"

She shook her head, causing that mop of curls to bounce and sway. "No," Lucy said, with a raspy note woven into her voice. "I think if I'm not careful, I'll be the one who's broken."

Abe reached out and grasped her wrist gently. He lifted her arm up, pulling back on the sleeve of her blouse to expose the scar. "I want to know the truth about this," Abe rumbled. His finger traced the jagged line, eliciting a shiver from Lucy.

"I told you I lived in South Carolina. What I left out was who I was when I was there, the past I was hiding from." Her lips pulled into a tight line. Shame, sadness, and… fear entered her gaze. "Our family owned a very successful plantation, but the emancipation changed things. My family was losing money quickly, and my father…"

"It's all right," Abe said. "Take your time."

"He tried to keep some slaves… hiding them from the law and forcing them to work in the indigo fields." Lucy wiped away a trail of tears that fell from her crystal blue eyes. "When I found out what he had done, I snuck the workers off the land. My father let the dogs loose on us, and I was bitten. The doc sewed me up, and I've been running ever since. I don't regret what I had to do to help them. God will forgive me for betraying my father to save those poor souls."

Abe leaned forward and planted a chaste kiss on her forehead. "You inspire me, Miss Baker," he whispered. "But, if you ask me, I think this isn't a story you should be hiding."

"A mercenary with a bleeding heart?" she chuckled with a warm smile upon her face. "I'll never find work in Texas again."

He toyed with a lock of her hair, avoiding the endless depths of blue in her eyes in fear of getting lost. "Working for the mayor out of guilt isn't ideal either. What happened between Ivan and his father was bound to happen, eventually."

"Perhaps. But I was alone after my annulment and I didn't know what else to do," Lucy explained. "The only skills I had were shooting and fighting, and neither of those are very profitable skills for a woman to have unless she's willing to swallow her pride and get her hands dirty."

"And how dirty are your hands, Miss Baker?" Abe held his breath as he waited for her answer.

"Not as dirty as the mayor thinks they are."

His brow furrowed in confusion, and he prodded a little more. "What's that supposed to mean?"

"I've killed no one, but I've done some bad things… things I had judged Ivan for doing in the past," she replied. "I'm not much of a proper lady or even a good woman, Mr. Delaney. I am what the world turned me into: a liar, a swindler, a gun for hire. That might not be enough for most folks around here, but I hope it's enough for you."

"Why would you care what I have to say?"

Lucy pushed up onto her tippy toes, trying to make up for the extreme height difference. "Because I like the way you look at me," she said so quietly that he could just barely make out the words.

Every fiber of his being trembled with the need to kiss Lucy Baker. Abe's hand moved to stroke her cheek, but he stopped himself short. Instead, he forced himself to step away from the temptation that stood before him. There was no doubt in his mind that Lucy Baker was under his skin. A realization that was far more frightening for the bounty hunter than he expected, for it gave him hope.

Hope for a future that was still far from his reach.

Chapter 6

Ivan clucked his tongue to get his horse moving. The mount trotted along the road obediently. Sunlight twinkled off the exposed metal of the saddle horn, illuminating Ivan's grim expression. Ladies batted their lashes as he passed by, brazenly adoring his handsome features in a way that had seemed improper just the year before. He flashed them a smile, but kept his head low in case someone recognized him. After all, he was wanted, not dead. The earthly temptations of this world still turned his head.

A pang of regret stole the smile from his lips, for no woman had ever replaced Lucy in his heart. She was strong, beautiful, and brave beyond reason. Losing her had changed everything for Ivan. The devastating consequences came almost instantly. Stiffness and pain radiated up his arm as the tendons in his hand cramped. He glanced down at the trembling appendage, the old injury serving as a constant reminder of the night his father had pinned his hand to the top of his desk.

Ivan's father had whipped barren land into shape, building a ranch he ran with an iron fist. But that ranch had slowly become so much more. It was a legacy—a legacy that Ivan never cared for. One he hadn't been willing to break Lucy's spirit to obtain.

"Where to, boss?" Victor asked, snapping Ivan from his thoughts.

"Head to the saloon. I'll be at the hotel." He clucked his tongue to urge his horse around the corner. Ivan hitched the mount to the post outside the hotel and wandered inside without a single person recognizing him. He supposed enough folks had come and gone in the past few weeks that he blended in more than he expected to. Even the man at the front desk failed to notice Ivan as he made his way up the stairs.

A small gallery overlooked the main floor of the hotel. Ivan caught sight of his target leaning over the banister with a cigar clenched between his teeth. The solicitor released a tendril of smoke as he exhaled. Ivan grabbed him by the back of his coat before the man could draw his next breath.

"What the—" They stumbled into the nearest room.

"You better have information for me, Jeremiah," Ivan sneered. "I've had you watching Ranger Greene and Sheriff Walker for nine days."

"There's nothin' to report!"

He checked as the solicitor fumbled to put out the cigar. "You expect me to believe they've given up hunting me? What I know could bring this town to its knees. My father wouldn't let that happen."

"Ranger Greene and the sheriff aren't on the case anymore," Jeremiah sputtered. "Your father hired someone else."

"Who?"

"I-I don't know."

Ivan curled his fingers around the grip of his pistol, ignoring the lingering pain in his hand. "I don't believe you," he growled. "Give me a name, or I'll spill your innards all over this floor."

The solicitor closed his eyes and prayed. His words rose in volume with each passing phrase, grating against Ivan's nerves until his patience snapped. Ivan pulled his gun from the holster and pressed the muzzle to the underside of Jeremiah's chin.

"I'm going to count to three," he stated. "If you don't tell me what I want to hear, I'll make good on my promise. Ready? One… Two…Thr—"

"Abraham Delaney!"

The name sounded familiar. "Go on."

"His partner… Tracker," Jeremiah sniveled. "They're bounty hunters working for your father."

"Anyone else?"

Jeremiah shook his head, but the sound of the hammer cocking forced his eyes and his mouth open. "A mercenary! I don't know the name, but they've… been hired to make sure you're brought in alive."

"There is nothing that would bring me more joy than to send their heads back to Ranger Greene on a silver platter. My father is playing a game with their lives," Ivan mused. "Will these bounty hunters get in my way?"

"No one can hide from Tracker. Don't let his Comanche blood fool you, there's a silver tongue hidden beneath it. And there isn't an outlaw left in the west who doesn't fear Abraham Delaney."

"Well, there's a first for everything," Ivan snickered. "I fear no mortal man."

"You don't understand… Abraham Delaney always catches his prey. The man is unlike anything you've ever seen before. He can look right into your soul and force you to confess your greatest sins."

Ivan wasn't convinced. "My sins are for God's ears only. A couple of bounty hunters and a mercenary are no worry for me. I've killed men more powerful than them."

He forced Jeremiah to his feet and led him back into the corridor. They walked toward the rear exit of the hotel, down the stairs, and along the back of the building. Ivan moved swiftly with the solicitor in his grasp until they arrived at City Hall.

"Just one more thing," he said as he lifted the gun to the center of Jeremiah's forehead. "You're fired."

The gun bucked in his hand after he pulled the trigger. A muffled pop resonated through the alleyway, barley loud enough to reach the street beyond the buildings that linked the narrow passage. Carriages rolled by without even slowing. Children played with a gangly mutt just a few yards away. Life continued on as the solicitor crumpled to the ground in a heap of useless limbs.

Ivan muttered under his breath and dragged the body into City Hall.

While the sheriff and Ranger Greene might not have been searching for him, Ivan thought Jeremiah would serve as a warning to anyone else who sought to take him down.

***

They rode along the canyon ridge not long after Ivan and his men left town. Abe stayed close to Lucy as they inched their way closer to the outlaw settlement. Tracker hovered a few feet away with a sullen expression on his face. Whatever Tracker had seen at that farmhouse had been enough to render him speechless, and that worried Abe.

"The annulment," Abe attempted to fill the silence, "how did you get Ivan to agree to it?"

"He didn't."

Abe frowned over at Lucy, and she explained further.

"When I told Ivan I wanted the annulment, he roughed me up and then disappeared for several days," she said. "His father still held power over the estate and had Ivan declared... unstable. It gave Jameson the right to request the annulment without Ivan when the judge saw the bruises. They granted the annulment under the condition I give up all rights to my possessions."

"It might have granted you freedom from Ivan, but it put you in the mayor's debt." The thought of anyone bringing harm to Lucy made him see red. Abe hated the way they tangled her up in the mayor's mess.

"I don't care."

"No?"

Lucy shook her head. "Debt is somethin' I can live with," she replied. "It's the guilt that keeps me awake at night."

Tracker rode up beside them suddenly. "We can't go through with the plan."

"We already discussed this," Abe grumbled. "Pretending to be—"

"Just listen," Tracker barked. "The mayor has been manipulating them for years. So far, we only know a false story of what happened. If we bring Miss Baker with us, then we have no leverage."

"Use Lucy to get the truth out of him?"

Tracker nodded. "The mayor sent her with us knowing we would eventually realize their connection. If he lied to us, then we have to assume he lied to Miss Baker about why she is here."

Abe pulled back on the reins and slowed his horse. "Tracker's right," he said to Lucy. "We could lead you into a trap. The mayor wants to keep something quiet, something Ivan might know."

"What is he hiding?" she asked.

"I don't know, but I intend to find out." He dug around in the saddle bag for a pair of binoculars and brought them up to his eyes. The small dials adjusted the sights until the Kingdom came into view. "All right. New plan."

"I hope this doesn't involve me goin'' home," Lucy quipped. "Because we both know how that argument is goin' to end."

Abe couldn't contain the slight smile that forced its way onto his lips. "You'll sneak inside and hunker down while Tracker and I demand an audience with this so-called king of outlaws. If we find ourselves pinned down, we'll need your help to get out of there. Cause a distraction and cover us as we retreat."

"Sounds simple enough," she sighed.

Abe looked to Tracker for his approval, and it surprised him to see his partner nod his head. For once, Lucy and

Tracker agreed on something. Abe hoped it was a start to repairing the damaged trust between them.

"Then it's final," he declared. "The goal here is to get as much information out of Ivan about the mayor as possible before we arrest him."

Lucy's warm gaze rivaled the heat of the blazing sun as it locked onto Abe's. He felt himself grow flustered beneath the onslaught of her attention. Tracker snorted in a teasing manner, wiggled his dark brows, and maneuvered ahead. Abe wanted to beg his partner not to leave him alone with the beautiful mercenary, but he kept his lips clamped shut.

"I understand." she chuckled. "I'm a complication you didn't ask for. Trust me, I didn't intend to tell you the truth or feel the way I do."

Abe tucked that information away for another time. He led his horse across the dried-up riverbed that cut through the landscape before they descended from the top of the canyon. Once the mount's hooves hit flat ground, Abe eased up on the reins and allowed the stallion to follow Tracker's mare. "If I hadn't figured out your connection to Ivan Lincoln, would you have tried to help him get free?"

"What?" Lucy balked. "I might not want to see him harmed, but that don't mean I want him free. Ivan deserves whatever punishment the law gives him. Whether it was me or his father who pushed him to the brink, it was his choice to kill those people. I see that now. Why would you ask me somethin' like that?"

"My partner raised a few questions where your loyalty was concerned," Abe responded. "And I wouldn't be honoring my friendship with Tracker if I let... whatever this is between you and me, get in the way of taking down your former husband."

"So… after all I've confessed, I'm still a person of interest?"

Abe had no choice but to confirm her accusations. He reached over and rested his hand on top of hers where it clutched the saddle horn. "Everyone is a person of interest until I know the truth," he replied. "There are too many lies and secrets for me to trust anyone other than myself and Tracker. I'm sorry…"

She gripped the brim of her hat and pulled it low to shield her eyes from the sun. Every slight movement Lucy made caused Abe's heart to beat dang near out of his chest. The soft, raspberry-stained color of her lips contrasted with the creamy hues of her skin. Tiny little scars peppered the otherwise flawless complexion. "Don't be sorry, Mr. Delaney," she sighed. "You have your reasons. But trust works both ways, I'm afraid, and I'm sure you have your own secrets you keep close and lies you tell. Just remember that when you're expectin' an honest answer from me."

"Lucy…" Abe removed his hand from the saddle horn and stared straight ahead. He rubbed the back of his neck before he replied, "You're holding on to a loyalty to Ivan that will do nothing but leave you filled with disappointment. While he still has a place in your heart and in your mind, do I even have a chance with you?"

***

The horses neighed and flicked their tails beside the small brook that trickled just a half mile from the Kingdom. Tracker wasn't sure what had changed between Abraham and Miss Baker, but an unusual tension lingered in the air, making the atmosphere uncomfortable. He watched their interactions for a bit longer before he strapped his bow to his back and headed on foot toward the town of outlaws.

A putrid scent of charred meat, sweat, and horse dung crawled up his nostrils when he got closer to the buildings. A trail of smoke reached for the sky as three riders approached the Kingdom from the east. Tracker remained out of sight, slipping behind a patch of shrubbery while keeping his eyes on the new arrivals. The man near the front moved like a graceful warrior… until Tracker noticed the familiar twitch in the man's hand.

The Reaper.

Ivan Lincoln lowered himself from the saddle near the stables and wiped the blood from his hands onto a rag. Tracker had never seen the man up close before. He was surprised by the very human features of someone called the Reaper. Abraham had been kind enough to explain to him why such a name was so significant to his people. And though his target had the face of a man, there was a darkness about the outlaw that sent a shiver down Tracker's spine.

It was as if death hovered nearby, lurking in the shadows until an opportunity presented itself. And he wasn't the only one affected by it, for it seemed the men in the small gang trembled with fear as their leader strolled past them.

"Where's the girl?" the Reaper asked.

"We tied her up in the barn. Want me to bring her inside?"

Tracker couldn't see who his target was talking to, but he followed a small path until he was less than a foot away from the exterior wall of the stables that were near the barn. A small window allowed him to peer into the unkept stalls where the animals were stored. At the center of the barn was a thick wooden post. Tracker hoisted himself up, swung his leg over the window frame, and lowered himself inside the barn without making a sound.

His moccasins shuffled across the hay-covered ground. An old cow lifted her head to stare at him as she chewed her cud. Tracker stroked his hand along the cow's side to keep the animal calm while he moved deeper into the barn. Bound to the wooden post was the young woman the outlaws mentioned. He heard her sniffle and crouched low, to not frighten her.

Wide, frightened green eyes stared at him from over the top of a scarf.

Tracker slowly lifted his hands to remove the gag from the woman's face. "My name is Tracker," he whispered. "I'm a bounty hunter, and I am going to get you out of here."

The woman nodded her head slowly.

Tracker pulled the knife from his belt and sawed through the ropes that kept her arms behind the post. The strain against her muscles must have caused the woman a lot of pain. She deflated against him the instant her binds were cut. Tracker slipped his knife between his teeth and lifted the woman into his arms.

Voices came from the other side of the barn door. Tracker had to hurry.

He propped the woman against the wall and lifted himself back through the window before offering her a hand. To his surprise, she wrapped her fingers around his wrist tightly. The tiny pinpricks of her nails scored his flesh. Tracker scooped her back up into his arms and hurried around the corner just as the barn door opened. He breathed heavily, creeping toward the edge of the Kingdom until he came upon an unhitched horse.

With no other options, Tracker helped the woman into the saddle.

He grabbed the reins and led the mount back toward the camp.

"My name is Emma," she said.

Tracker replied with a wordless grunt and a nod of acknowledgement.

"Thank you for saving me, Mr. Tracker. I thought I was going to die in that place."

"Why did the Reaper take you?" he asked. Tracker kept his gaze pointed toward the ground so he didn't offend her, even as his question was spoken sharply.

"He killed everyone." Her voice cracked on the last word. Whatever happened to Emma still seemed to be fresh in her mind. "I was so afraid. The jewels and the money meant nothing to me, but my father... the servants... it was evil, Mr. Tracker. Pure evil. I reckon the Reaper took me simply because there was no one around to tell him he couldn't."

Tracker reached into his pocket and fished out his bandanna. He held it out for Emma to dry her tears with, but it did not hurt him when she rejected his offer. "I am sorry about your family," he heard himself say. "There is no need to be afraid anymore. My partner and I will take care of the Reaper. He cannot hurt you."

"So… you really are a bounty hunter?" she asked in disbelief.

He snorted bitterly, shaking his head at the sheer absurdity of the idea despite living with the reality of it. "It was either become a bounty hunter or become the hunted. Some days, the two are more similar than I would like, but knowing I am on the side of justice makes it worth the trouble. No peace is won without sacrifice. If I am the one to pay the price, then I'm glad it is for the right reasons."

Chapter 7

Abe wanted nothing more than to send Lucy back to town with Emma in tow, but the stubborn set of Lucy's shoulders left no room for argument. He grumbled under his breath as he packed up the horses. Tracker's instinct to rescue the hostage had been correct, but Abe was tempted just to tie all three of them down and deal with the Reaper on his own. There were too many liabilities, too many chances for the meeting to turn sour.

He waited beside a pathetic little tree, tapping his foot impatiently against the exposed roots that poked up from the dry earth. Tracker sent Emma back to San Antonio with a letter for Ranger Greene and instructions to send help if they didn't return in three days. Abe waved the young woman goodbye as she left the camp, but he kept his mind focused.

Once they watered and fed the horses, Abe and Tracker rode toward the entrance to the Kingdom. Their entire plan rested on his blind faith and fragile trust in Lucy. He hoped she had followed the path marked by Tracker when he went to survey the land. Under normal circumstances, Abe would have admired her pig-headedness and brazen attitude, but he feared those qualities were going to get her hurt someday.

"We're here," Tracker announced.

Sentries paced along the perimeter, wearing the mark of the Reaper on their jackets. Abe approached the guards without hesitation, something made easier by his partner being within arm's reach. He tipped his hat to the men as they stopped in their tracks. One guard approached Abe's horse and eyed the guns tied down to the saddle warily.

"We're here to see the Reaper," Abe grumbled. "He available?"

"The king ain't acceptin' visitors."

"Too bad," Tracker snapped before Abe could speak.

Abe lifted his hand to keep his partner's anger at bay. He stretched languidly, keeping his eyes on the sentry with a hand on his gun belt. "He'll make an exception for me," Abe replied. "Tell him his hostage is on her way back to the city, and I'm sure he'll want to speak with the man responsible."

The second sentry dashed out of sight. Tracker chuckled deeply beside Abe as he picked at a loose thread along the leg of his trousers. Loud, booming voices came from the large house he assumed belonged to Ivan Lincoln. A smile appeared on Abe's face when the sentry returned to allow them entrance into the Kingdom.

Men appeared to take their weapons and horses, but Abe refused. Tracker challenged any man brave enough to try to take his bow. In the end, they agreed to an escort at gunpoint over surrendering their possessions. The ride through the Kingdom revealed just how unsavory a town run by outlaws could get.

Gambling, violence, and all-around mayhem ensued.

They arrived at the home of Ivan "the Reaper" Lincoln. Abe ordered Tracker to stay with the horses, and his partner complied. He knocked on the front door. It opened with a squeak, revealing to Abe the face of his target.

"You stole my cook," Ivan muttered.

Abe took a moment and observed the king of outlaws. A perfectly tailored suit covered a muscular physique that was more like the mayor's than Abe expected. Regal features set Ivan apart from the surrounding criminals, but no amount of careful breeding could hide the cold eyes of a killer. It was like staring into the gaze of a shark.

"Emma told me you killed her father and the workers on the farm," Abe said with a shrug. "She didn't seem to know why, so I would like an answer."

"Who are you?"

Abe ignored the question. He leaned forward and continued to antagonize Ivan, trying to get him to show the insanity that hid behind a carefully crafted facade. "Was it just another one of your tantrums, Ivan? Your father told me all about you."

Cold-blooded hatred swarmed Ivan's gaze. He grabbed the front of Abe's shirt and dragged him into the house. Abe shot his partner a quick look to keep him calm, but Tracker followed them inside, anyway.

"You know nothing about my father!" the outlaw snarled. "He sent you, didn't he? You are the bounty hunters he hired to—"

"Look at yourself. Just as mad as he said you would be." Abe watched the cracks in the mask appear as Ivan fought to control his rage. The twitch in the outlaw's hand worsened with his heightened emotions.

"My father is weak! He basked in the glory of my accomplishment and kept me in the shadows," Ivan claimed. "I did everything. I took a cattle baron and turned him into a mayor, but all he could see was my failure…"

Tracker snatched Ivan away from Abe.

"You mean Lucy?" Abe asked.

Abe saw the change in Ivan immediately. Gone was the unbridled rage, and in its place was a look filled with so much longing it made Abe pity the outlaw. But along with the longing was something else… sadness. The sort of sadness that came from a loss too painful to bear.

"Ivan… Lucy got an annulment because she couldn't live with being the wife of a murderer."

"You're lying," the outlaw hissed. "Lucy died the night I left San Antonio."

Abe was struck silent by Ivan's words. He could hardly fathom that Mayor Jameson would have told his son such a horrendous lie. "Lucy is very much alive, Ivan. Your father used her guilt over your fall into madness to turn her into his personal mercenary."

"No… no, that isn't true."

"She's waiting for my signal," Abe revealed. He placed his hand on Tracker's shoulder, maneuvering his partner out of the way in case Ivan lost control. "You have a choice. Come with me and tell me everything you know about the crimes your father has committed. I'll let you talk with Lucy, I'll give you the option of a fair trial, and I'll make sure your father can't use you to clear his name. You have my word on that."

"Or?"

"Or you resist," he sighed. "And my partner and I take you in by any means necessary."

Ivan Lincoln burst into laughter so maniacally it made Abe shift uncomfortably on his feet. The outlaw clutched his middle, collapsing into a fit of giggles that belied the darkness of his reputation. "You almost had me going there."

"Pardon me?" Abe asked in confusion.

"I know who you are, Abraham Delaney, and my father is a heartless pig, but he isn't cunning enough to devise a plan that ends with me dead." Ivan moved over to a desk that sat off to the side and opened the drawer. He dropped a familiar document on the floor in front of Abe and Tracker, an impish grin appearing on his face. "You can't touch me."

Abe crouched down long enough to pick up the contract that held his and Tracker's signatures. "Where did you get this?"

"There was a loose tongue wagging in the city, so I cut it off," Ivan snorted. "My father made a mistake sending you after me. He knows it would be best to keep me quiet, and yet he continues to give me reasons to expose his little box of horrors."

"Contract or not, my partner and I will not let a murderer like you go free." He nodded his head toward Tracker, who notched an arrow in his bow so fast it barely made a sound.

Ivan Lincoln continued to look unfazed by their threats.

Abe continued, "The folks living in this town might see you as some sort of king, but all I see is a frightened little boy trying to impress his pa. You never should have come back to Texas, Ivan."

"I am not my father's puppet any longer!" Ivan slammed his hand down onto the desk. "Say what you want, bounty hunter, but I'm the key to freeing the west from the chains of civility. My wife died nine years ago. Using her name against me will get you nowhere."

Abe lifted his fingers to his mouth and whistled so sharply it caused his ears to ring. A moment later, the window slid open, and Lucy climbed through the opening.

Ivan's jaw dropped.

He blinked rapidly, trying to banish the hallucination that appeared before him. Lucy… his precious, innocent Lucy stood so close he almost believed he could reach out and touch her. Beautiful features were pinched into a tight frown. But she was alive. Ivan resisted the urge to run to her. The realization that she did not try to reach out to him caused shame to burn in his gut. "I thought you were dead," he said finally.

Lucy shook her head. "No. Not dead."

"But you're not my wife anymore?"

"Your father convinced a judge to grant me an annulment," she explained. "You had disappeared, Ivan. People were saying you had gone mad. Now I see they were right."

He took a step toward Lucy and heard a pistol cock. Ivan's gaze flickered over to where Abraham Delaney's gun lifted into view. Tracker moved to Lucy's side as if she needed protection… protection from *him,* of all people.

Something nagged in the back of his head. A memory crawled out of the darkest depth. Ivan suddenly saw himself standing over Lucy as she looked up at him with tears in her eyes, a hand-sized bruise darkening her shoulder.

Ivan stumbled, shaken by the force of the memory. "I hurt you..."

"You're sick," she said in that tone that made him want to run away like a scolded child. The disappointment... The pity in her eyes was almost too much for Ivan to handle.

"So you and these men are here to save me from myself? Is that it?" Ivan asked, leaving none of the bitterness out of his voice.

"I'm here to help you, yes. But I'm also here to absolve myself of the guilt that has tormented me over the years." Lucy approached him with caution. She cupped his jaw in a touch so gentle it made him shiver. "Surrender yourself, Ivan. I know the man who saved me from my father is still somewhere inside of you. Please."

He grasped her hand and breathed deeply, basking in the warm scent of her perfume that had haunted his dreams. "I'll do it for you, Lucy."

She graced him with a smile. "Thank you."

Ivan looked over at Abraham Delaney. "I'll tell you everything you need to know about my father," he said. "But I want your word that I'll get leniency."

"I can't make that decision," the bounty hunter replied. "You're lucky there's even a trial in the cards for you because of your father's influence. Giving a murderer like you leniency would destroy everything I believe in."

"But I killed no one who didn't give me a choice." The lie rolled off his tongue easier than it should have. "My father has been controlling me since the day I learned how to walk, forcing me to do his dirty work."

"Am I supposed to believe your father ordered a hit on that farmer and his family, too?" Delaney snapped. "Or that Ranger Greene would lie about you killing those deputies?"

"My father is a lot more powerful than he would have you believe." Ivan dropped Lucy's hand and rubbed his eyes. "This gang is his. This land is his… The blood on my hands is his. All I've done is follow orders."

"Then you shouldn't have a problem proving your innocence." Abraham Delaney tossed a pair of handcuffs to Lucy. "Arrest him," he ordered. "He may have surrendered, but I'm not taking any chances."

Ivan held his arms out willingly, eager to show them just how docile he could be if he wanted to… In fact, Ivan could have told them everything. He could have exposed his father and run for the hills, but he stayed. He stayed to see just how far Abraham Delaney wanted to play his little game.

Chapter 8

Tracker felt uneasy.

He walked ahead of the others, guiding them out the back of the house and toward the wall that surrounded the Reaper's home. Capturing their target had been too easy. Tracker wondered if Abraham was thinking along the same lines, for his partner slowed once they made their way through the gate.

"The tongue-wagger you mentioned," Abraham started. "Does he have a name?"

The Reaper smiled like the heartless criminal Tracker knew he was and said, "Just know I put an end to one of my father's crooked solicitors. He framed me a few years back, and I was just defending myself."

Tracker stiffened. He recalled handing over a copy of the contract to one person only. "Jeremiah Wilson. He was the solicitor you silenced?"

The Reaper went quiet.

Tracker took his silence as an admission of guilt. "This was never about exposing your father," he said accusingly. "This is about taking out anyone who could prove that you—"

The shackles that had been secured around the Reaper's wrists dropped to the dirt with a loud clatter before Tracker could react. He reached out for Ivan, but it was too late. Pain exploded across the back of his head, and his vision went dark. Tracker hit the dirt, gasping as he tried to clear the black spots from his vision.

Abraham tackled the outlaw and they slammed into the wall. Ivan slammed his fist into Abraham's ribcage, causing the bounty hunter's legs to buckle. Tracker climbed to his feet. He attempted to restrain their prisoner, but Ivan fought with a skill that baffled his rattled mind. Fists flew past his face. Even Lucy tried to grab a hold of the outlaw.

Ivan broke free from Abraham's crushing grip and landed a brutal punch against his jaw. Tracker lunged toward the outlaw, scrambling to catch him before he could make a run for it. His grip slipped, and Ivan climbed over the wall. Abraham unholstered his pistol, squeezed the trigger, and shot Ivan in the leg. The outlaw let out a pained shriek that made Tracker's head feel like someone had hammered a nail between his eyes.

Their target limped behind a large crate and rang an alarm bell. Tracker's stomach clenched painfully.

Dogs barked and armed guards shouted a warning just before bullets pelted the wall right beside his head. He rolled off to the side, leaped over a rock that protruded from the ground, and grabbed Abraham by the back of his shirt. Tracker dragged his partner out of the line of fire. Bullets sprayed the ground. Bandits hollered out slurs that made his blood run cold.

"You fool!" Lucy screamed at her former husband as he crawled onto the safety of his porch. "We were your last hope, and you threw it away!"

Ivan wiped his sleeve across a bloodied lip and grinned. "There's no hope for me, Lucy. This is my world now, and I'm not sure I want the three of you in it."

"You're only doin' exactly what your father wants!" she roared, but it was useless.

That cold detachment was back. Ivan pointed toward the wall and yelled, "Light 'em up, boys!"

Another wave of bullets punched through the wall and hit the trees that surrounded them. Tracker pressed his back against the trunk of the tree. Abraham crouched behind a stone with his eyes trained on Lucy.

Tracker cursed when he realized the foolish woman had placed herself right in the middle of the chaos. "She didn't secure the cuffs," he said pointedly.

"I checked them myself, they were secure."

"How did he remove them, then?" He forced down the bile that bubbled up the back of his throat. "They made those shackles of pure iron."

"Must have been something he learned over the years," his partner argued. "Right now, we have to focus on fighting our way out of here."

Abraham motioned for Tracker to round up the horses before he sprinted toward Lucy. Tracker groaned as he stood up, breathing roughly through his nose. He touched the back of his head and grimaced at the sight of blood. Everything blurred as the world shifted sideways. Tracker fought to stay on his feet and shuffled along the wall toward the mounts. Pain spread along his skull, throbbing with the frantic beat of his heart.

Trembling fingers readied an arrow.

He released the bowstring and sent the arrow soaring toward an outlaw blocking his path. The gun in the man's hand discharged. Loud gunshots rang through the air, mingling with the sounds of gun fire just a few feet from where Tracker stood. Abraham called his name, but there was nothing he could do for them as he made his way over to the hitching post. His partner's stallion tossed his mane and whinnied.

Tracker could almost feel the fear radiating off the creature. He untied the horses and climbed into the saddle. His head swam, lolling forward as a wave of nausea swept through him. And still the fighting raged on. Abraham returned fire. The outlaws scattered, running for cover as Tracker rode hard back to his partner's side.

Lucy flipped the lever on her rifle and ejected the empty shell before reloading. Her movements were swift and precise, shooting with a lethal accuracy that impressed Tracker. Lucy must have caught sight of his approach. She peered out from behind her cover and emptied the rounds in her firearm. Tracker could reach them as the Reaper's men evaded her shots. Abraham hoisted himself up into the saddle before he pulled Lucy in front of him. Tracker noticed Abraham had used his own body to shield her from harm.

It spooked the horses.

Abe's mount shot through the trees like a gator was snapping at his ankles. An outlaw jumped up and latched onto the saddle. Tracker spun around in his seat and fired his bow. The arrow hit its mark, striking the man in his arm and forcing him to release his hold on Abe's horse. Lucy pulled the pistol from Abe's holster.

"Two riders are following!" she screamed into his ear.

The kickback from the guns jostled Abe as he tried to steer the horse out of the line of fire. Tracker notched another arrow. Only the startled shout that followed the whistle of the arrow told Abe that, once again, his partner's aim was true. He snapped the reins and spurred on his horse as Tracker turned back around.

A row of spikes blocked the path up ahead.

Abe bit back a curse and veered off to the right at the last possible second. The rider behind them didn't have time to correct his mistake. A cloud of dust billowed around them, obscuring Abe's vision momentarily. "Is he still after us?" he asked.

Lucy shook her head and returned his pistols to their holsters. "We lost them, but that doesn't mean more won't come. Dang it! I can't believe Ivan could be so stupid."

Abe clenched his jaw until the muscle in his neck twitched. He held Lucy against his chest, praying to God his horse was fast enough to dodge the bullets that still whizzed past his ear. She clung to him. Tiny whimpers escaped her lips every few heartbeats as her tears soaked the shoulder of his shirt. He tried to block out the sniffles and the hiccups, the winded breaths and the moments where her fingers would squeeze his arm as if the pain of seeing Ivan's true colors was too much to bear. He ached for her loss, but he couldn't help but selfishly wondered if she could finally let go of Ivan Lincoln.

Tracker's horse slowed near the edge of the valley that surrounded the Kingdom. Abe glanced over his shoulder and saw that none of the outlaws had given chase. He followed

Tracker's lead toward the water. They dismounted behind a rock formation that blocked out the sun. Abe wanted to collapse the second his feet hit the ground. Every bone in his body ached after trading punches with Ivan.

Lucy slid off the saddle and into his arms. Her hands brushed over his chest before circling around his back. "Are you all right? Did you get hurt?" She fussed over him longer until Abe couldn't take it anymore. He caught her hands and cradled them.

"I'm fine, Lucy."

But Tracker wasn't.

Abe felt as if his greatest nightmare had become a reality when Tracker toppled over. He raced to his partner's side, with Lucy on his heels. They dropped to their knees beside Tracker, and Abe saw a bullet had grazed his partner's thigh deeply. A dark stain spread across the deer hide of Tracker's trousers. "Get a fire started and fetch some water," he ordered Lucy.

She hurried to fulfil his demands, collecting dry kindling for the fire before Abe lifted Tracker off the ground. He carried his partner closer to the river and splashed water onto Tracker's face to keep him awake. Tracker's eyes shot open. He dug his fingers into the dirt beneath him as Abe used his knife to cut away the sodden cloth from his leg.

"W-what happened?" Tracker asked.

"They shot you while we were retreating. Lie still."

"Lucy...?"

"She's fine," Abe said as he applied pressure to the wound. "You didn't notice the bullet hitting your leg while you were in the saddle?"

"No. I was too busy worrying about my head." Tracker hissed when Abe prodded along the back of his head.

"Ivan whacked you pretty good," he grumbled. "Got any liquor in that flask of yours?"

"This is not the time for drinking, Abraham."

"It's to sterilize your wound while I patch you up," Abe chuckled. Though Tracker's English was near perfect, there were still a few things that eluded the man.

Lucy crouched down and struck two stones together. Sparks ignited the kindling. Smoke oozed from between the pyramid of sticks until an unbearable warmth bloomed around them. Sweat dripped down Abe's temples as he stuck his knife into the embers.

Tracker watched his actions with concern in his gaze. "On second thought… maybe I would like a drink."

"Sorry, brother," Abe chuckled. "I need you to stay conscious in case that head injury of yours is more serious than it looks. Lucy? Grab my kit out of my saddle bag, will you?"

She brushed her hands off on her skirts and retrieved a small leather parcel. "Is he goin' to be all right?" Lucy asked softly. "That wound looks pretty bad."

"We'll do what we can for him, but he'll need to see a doctor when we get to town. Infection could set in out here, and I…" Abe couldn't finish the thought.

Losing Tracker wasn't an option for him. Without his partner, he was as good as dead. The fear that gnawed at his insides continued to fester while he worked on getting Tracker back on his feet.

Time passed slowly until Abe saw nothing, heard nothing, and felt nothing.

The sun set beyond the horizon, washing the land in hues of tangerine and violet. Shadows closed in around the camp as Tracker eventually fell unconscious from the pain. Abe had done all he could for his partner. He stood up and walked over to the water to wash the blood from his hands. Lucy did her best to clean up Tracker. She adjusted his clothing to maintain his modesty and used a wet handkerchief to remove the dirt from his face.

"Thank you," Abe said. He cleared his throat and swallowed past the lump of emotion that caused his voice to crack. "Most people wouldn't show such care."

"I think I've proven I'm not most people."

Chapter 9

Gray Post, Texas

Tracker awakened to find they had strapped him down to a bed. He flexed his arms and frowned down at the restraints that held him captive. The door in front of the bed opened. A doctor stepped inside the room with Abraham at his side. The smile on his partner's face was a relief.

"Is it safe to assume no one died?" he asked to no one in particular, not expecting an actual answer.

"You gave us quite the scare, partner. Lucy insisted we stop at a town nearby to get you some help." Abe moved to sit beside the bed. "Dr. Morton here agreed to treat you if you were restrained."

At least the doctor had enough brains to look ashamed of his prejudice. Tracker wasn't so ignorant to think the violent reputation his people garnered wouldn't follow him everywhere.

"When do we leave?" Tracker croaked. He licked his dry lips to alleviate the dryness of his mouth. Abe was kind enough to help him take a sip of water—even if it was out of a finger-smudged glass.

"We'll leave as soon as you can stand up without falling over. How about that?" his partner teased. "I'm glad you're all right, Tracker. Lord knows I wouldn't have made it without you."

Tracker scowled at Abraham. "Please tell me we will not talk about our feelings now."

Abraham's startled laughter seemed to brighten the room. Suddenly, things seemed less dire than they had a moment ago. Tracker even sat still as the nervous doctor checked over his thick and then the wound on the back of his head. Not long after Dr. Morton finished up, Lucy crept into the room shyly.

"I am still not sure if we can trust you," Tracker said to the mercenary woman. "But I hope you see now that the Reaper is not the man you married."

Tears glistened in Lucy's eyes as she said, "Life makes fools of us all, eventually. I realize I can't save Ivan, that he doesn't deserve to be free."

The sadness and heartbreak he sensed within her was more akin to losing a loved one to death than a wife fearing for the sanity and freedom of her former husband. Perhaps in some ways the Ivan Lincoln she had known died in her mind, leaving behind only the outlaw known as the Reaper. When Abraham grabbed Lucy's hand to offer her comfort, Tracker envied him.

He envied his partner's newfound pursuit of love and happiness. Tracker remembered it wasn't so long ago Abraham had forsaken the idea of marriage and a family. Has Lucy given Abraham the hope he so desperately needs? Tracker wondered. "Neither of you were injured?" he asked.

It was Abraham who answered, "I broke two fingers, but we're fine other than that."

"Have you heard about any movement at the Kingdom?" he questioned. "It's only a matter of time before he tries to hunt us down."

The expression on Abraham's face worried Tracker. "We have to prepare to be questioned by the mayor when we return to San Antonio."

"Prepare how?"

"To lie," Abraham explained. "The mayor is crooked, and he blackmailed Lucy and Ivan, used them as weapons to get elected last time. For all we know, he could use the same tactics against Ranger Greene."

"What do you suggest then?" Tracker felt a tug on his arm and realized Lucy had untied the restraints.

Abraham answered, "We tell Mayor Jameson that Ivan was killed in the fight at the Kingdom. I think we'll be able to at least get him to confess to his own crimes."

"That still leaves Ivan free to do as he pleases without repercussion." Tracker's arms were freed from the binds. A damp cloth soothed the skin on his arms the straps had rubbed raw. "We could feed the legend who makes him so dangerous."

"It's our only option," Abraham stressed. "Someone isn't telling us the complete story, and I want to get the truth out of them.'

Lucy replaced the rag in the washbasin and helped Tracker sit up. "Abe's right," she said. "If Ivan thought I was dead, there's no telling what the mayor has lied about to him."

"When I met with Jeremiah, we talked about the contract." Tracker felt their prying gazes on him as he spoke.

"He told me we would need someone with authority to help us. I think he was implying there is no proper authority in the city."

Lucy glanced between Abraham and Tracker. "There isn't."

Tracker sensed a change in his partner. Abraham jumped to his feet and paced around his room. "The sheriff," he said, as if that explained everything. "Ranger Greene said Ivan always knew when they would make an arrest, how they intended to transport him, and that he would escape, right? That's because the sheriff has been leaking information to Ivan from the inside."

"Why get his own deputies killed?" Tracker inquired.

Neither Abraham nor Lucy had an answer.

Tracker huffed and tried to stand up on his own. The pain in his thigh was accompanied by a tightness caused by the sutures. He clumsily stumbled over to his things. It was obvious Abraham had attempted to get him new clothing, no doubt assuming the stains would trigger him. "Let's get out of here, then. This case will not get solved with us sitting around, waiting for me to heal."

"I'm with you, partner."

***

The Kingdom
San Antonio, Texas

Thousands of dollars' worth of damage to his property. Fury overcame Ivan. He slammed his fists into the exterior wall of his home over and over until he felt his knuckles tighten from swelling. Only pain cleared his mind, and he was almost grateful for the bullet wound in his leg.

Ivan hobbled into his house and up the stairs, one step at a time. He tried his best to ignore the holes in the upholstery and window trimmings left behind by stray bullets. His home was ruined, that much was clear to him, but it was Lucy's betrayal that hurt him the most.

She had willingly sided with Abraham Delaney and his partner, Tracker. It was something he wasn't sure he could ever forgive her for. Helping his father collect debts and roughing up a few people was nothing. Helping the law, however, that was something that enraged his soul.

"I want them found!" Ivan yelled as he limped down the corridor that led to his bedchamber. He slowly made his way over to the wardrobe tucked in the corner of his room. The wound in his calf burned like nothing he had ever felt before. Luckily, the bullet hadn't snapped the bone or torn open an artery. Abraham Delaney and Tracker had signed their own death warrants when they walked into his kingdom.

Not only had they belittled him, used his precious Lucy against him, and tried to get him to surrender, but they had ruined his favorite suit. Ivan gritted his teeth as he peeled away the layers of clothing from his body. Victor stood in the doorway with a sullen expression on his face.

"They'll run right back to the mayor," Victor guessed. "That contract won't keep you safe if your father thinks you betrayed him."

"Relax, Vic." Ivan plopped down onto the corner of his bed and looked down at the lopsided sutures on his leg. "Abraham Delaney won't say a word to my father. He wouldn't admit he failed to capture me so soon."

"You think they'll attack again?"

He nodded his head in response to Victor's question. "They would be foolish not to," he said. "They've seen how few men we have and what little resources we keep. Eventually, we'll have to leave the safety of our walls to get food and drink, right?"

"An ambush?"

"No," Ivan replied. "That's too deceptive for a man like Delaney." He snapped his fingers, and a chambermaid appeared behind Victor. The meek woman ducked her head as she squeezed past his right-hand man. Her flushed cheeks and quivering shoulders caught his attention. "What's your name?"

"Marlene," she whispered.

"Good to meet you, Marlene. Do you visit the city?" Ivan watched as she bobbed her head subtly. "That's perfect. I have a message I want you to take to Ranger Greene when you go to the city."

The maid curtsied and scurried from the room.

Ivan slowly dressed in a fresh suit before he followed Victor down to the dining room. His men sat around the long rectangular table. Each one of them had disappointed him greatly.

"How many guards do we have left?" he asked Victor.

"Lucy wound Ty, chasing after Delaney. Lou was killed by the Comanche near the stables, and an arrow struck Walt in the shoulder. That leaves only three more guards on their feet for patrol tonight."

Ivan pulled out a chair and joined his men at the table, eager to rest his injured leg. "We can't just sit around and wait for Abraham Delaney to come up with a plan of attack. I say we teach them a lesson." He reached beneath the table and massaged a cramp out of his leg. The outlaws around the table waited patiently for him to continue. "I want Victor to watch Delaney. Keep eyes on him at all times, make him feel the pressure."

"What about the rest of us?" Jasper asked.

"You and Wade will follow the tracks left behind in their retreat," Ivan ordered. "Kill anyone who helped them along the way. People need to learn the price of treason. The rest of you need to fix the damage done to my home!" His voice rang through the dining room, causing the hardened criminals to jump in their seats.

They scattered like cockroaches when he slammed his fist on the table. Chairs scraped across the floor, and the sound of fading footfalls reached his ears. Ivan sighed as he deflated in his seat. Victor stood beside him with a scowl, pinching his features into a mask of ugliness.

"Out with it!"

"I think it's time we take care of the ranger," Victor suggested. "If we remove Greene from the equation, it'll leave your father with no one left to chase you down. He'll be forced to do it himself."

Ivan smiled and stood up from his chair slowly. He wrapped his arms around Victor and let out a shout of excitement as he clapped his comrade on the back. "Brilliant! Getting rid of Greene will humiliate Delaney and leave my father vulnerable."

"Are you going to kill him?" Victor asked.

Ivan pulled away from the hug and leaned back against the table. The servants carried in platters of food to set the table. He cast them a mean glare and sent them running back to the kitchen. They couldn't afford for anyone to hear their conversation, especially the two gossiping maids he acquired recently after taking them from their families. Sometimes death wasn't the answer to his problems—sometimes money got him further than violence ever could.

"No. I'll make him an offer he can't afford to reject. With his third child on the way, I doubt my father's wages are keeping him comfortable." He ran his fingers through his freshly cut hair, wincing when he felt several large bumps against his skull.

"Extortion?"

"An offer of employment," Ivan clarified. "Under the threat of immense pain and torture, of course. We are outlaws, after all."

Chapter 10

Everything was quiet when Abe and the others arrived in San Antonio. Several shops had been boarded up and abandoned along the edge of the city. Folks whispered as they moseyed along the sidewalks, swathed in black. Abe waved down a deputy who nailed a wanted poster to the outside of the saloon. "Excuse me, deputy. Could you fill us in on what happened here?"

"We have found a body at City Hall," the deputy answered. "A solicitor by the name of Jeremiah Wilson, I believe. Folks seem to think it was the Reaper and his gang, but no one saw it happen."

Abe felt Tracker's anger as if it were his own. Though Tracker and Jeremiah Wilson had a complicated history, it was clear the news of his acquaintance's death affected Tracker greatly. Abe even wondered if Tracker blamed himself for the solicitor getting killed so soon after revealing Ivan Lincoln's hideout.

"You all right?" Abe asked quietly. His words barely made it over the sound of rattling carriage wheels and clicking hooves on the road.

"I will be fine when we get some genuine answers," Tracker replied.

Abe thanked the deputy before he carried on toward the hotel near the mayor's office. They barely had time to set their bags down before a knock came at the door.

It was a lawman, who stood with a cigarette hanging off his lip and a mean furrow to his brow. "Mayor wants to see you," he announced. "It's urgent matters."

Abe took in the man's appearance. If not for the sheriff's badge pinned to a striped vest, Abe would have slammed the door in his face. "And you are?" the bounty hunter asked, watching as the man spat on the floor with no care for manners.

"Sheriff Walker."

"Funny how our paths haven't crossed until now," Abe said bitterly. "Do you mind telling me how Jeremiah Wilson was murdered right under your nose, Sheriff?"

Tracker grabbed Abe's arm and gave him a look that quelled his temper almost instantly. He had to keep a level head if they wanted to catch Ivan Lincoln.

"Tell the mayor—"

"I ain't an errand boy, Mr. Delaney," Sheriff Walker huffed. "Got somethin' to say to the mayor, do it yourself."

Abe was about two seconds away from giving the sheriff a piece of his mind. Either Walker was stupid enough to think his badge made him invincible, or the folks in San Antonio had let him get away with enough foolishness that he thought no one would stand up to him. Abe was exhausted. There were too many egos getting in the way of his job. He opened his mind to speak, but Lucy stepped in front of him.

She squared her shoulders and glared up at the sheriff. "How much is Ivan payin' you, Thomas?"

The color drained from the sheriff's face. He went white as a sheet. "That's a dangerous accusation to be tossin' around, Lucy," Sheriff Walker growled. "You know I got more cause than anybody to want the Reaper gone."

Lucy shook her head before replying, "Some things ain't addin' up. Mr. Delaney and his partner want to know how Ivan always seems to be one step ahead of the law… and why you never seem to be around when the shootin' starts."

Abe smiled over Lucy's shoulder as Sheriff Walker babbled nervously. There was no proper explanation, just thoughtless mumbling that came as the result of being surprised. Lucy wasn't exactly tactful or particularly good with words, but her methods were effective. Abe shut the door before the sheriff's head exploded out of sheer anger and frustration.

"He's dirty," Tracker said. "What sort of sheriff sits around doing nothing while they slaughter his deputies?"

"I think Tracker is right," Lucy added. "I've been tryin' to come up with a reason why the sheriff is never around when Ivan and his men show up."

Abe nodded his head. He understood their suspicions, for he had a few similar ones himself. It was time for Sheriff Walker to take some accountability. "All right. This is what we'll do," Abe began. "Tracker and I will go to this meeting with the mayor. We'll try to get some answers. I want you, Lucy, to search the sheriff's desk and try to find anything tying him to the Reaper."

Tracker limped over to the window and peered down at the street. "Search his home as well," he said. "The sheriff is cunning enough to hide his secrets somewhere the ranger will not look."

Abe washed his face and changed his shirt before he helped Tracker down to the mayor's office. He wished Lucy good luck, but he doubted she needed it. After he saw her fight at the Kingdom, it convinced Abe she could take care of herself. He was just glad she was on his side instead of Ivan's.

Tracker shrugged off his help when they reached the entrance to the mayor's office. Abe watched as his partner gathered every ounce of his strength to appear as if he wasn't in excruciating pain. He knew very well that Tracker was standing with nothing more than sheer willpower. "You ready for this?" Abe asked his partner. "We can make them wait another day. Let them stew."

"I want this over with, Abraham." Tracker reached for the door handle and pushed inside the dimly lit office. Sheriff Walker, Mayor Jameson, and Ranger Greene greeted them with a simple nod of acknowledgement from the other side of the room.

Four sets of eyes stared at Tracker as he sat himself in the chair across from the mayor's desk. He held his breath to keep from wincing at the pain that still coursed through his body. Abraham stood beside the chair, taking the spotlight off Tracker. If only for a few seconds. The lawmen seemed to take a particular interest in him, and it made Tracker .

"Thank you for meetin' with us, gentlemen," Mayor Jameson said finally. Tracker's eyes burned as the enormous man blew smoke rings from between pursed lips, filling the room with a thick fog. Mayor Jameson's demeanor would have appeared relaxed to an ordinary person—Tracker saw a man on the brink of losing everything he worked for.

Abraham placed his hand on the back of Tracker's chair and dropped his voice to a rumbling timbre. "One of the sheriff's new deputies informed us that they have murdered a solicitor in our absence," he muttered. "Forgive me for being a little unfriendly when I'm having trouble figuring out how the Reaper sneaked past the three of you and a handful of deputies."

"I don't like your implications, Mr. Delaney." Mayor Jameson's response wasn't surprising to Tracker. However, the confusion that eclipsed the suspicion in Ranger Greene's eyes seemed strange.

"Excuse me, Mr. Mayor," Abraham chuckled. "I meant no offense. You and I got off on the wrong side of things, but I'm still willing to work with you… if you're willing to tell the truth, that is."

"I have been nothin' if not honest in our exchanges."

Tracker tried and failed to hold back a snarl. His lip curled in disgust. The mayor was just like every other politician he had come across. They valued nothing above power… even their own humility. "That is not what we discovered," Tracker argued. "Our conversation with the Reaper was very enlightening."

"It painted an entirely different picture," Abraham added helpfully. He walked around Tracker's chair and stood before the enormous desk in the office. "You saw potential in Ivan from the start, but you were a heartless man, incapable of loving even your own flesh and blood."

"I loved my son!" Ashes fell from the mayor's cigar, dusting the tops of the papers that sat in front of him. "I only wanted what was best for Ivan. I sacrificed everythin' to make sure that he could have a brilliant future!"

Tracker shook his head and replied, "There was no future for him if he was also to be your sacrifice."

Hatred, raw and untamed, snapped in the mayor's eyes. But Tracker didn't stop there.

"You turned your son into a killer, used him as a steppingstone to pave the way for your success," he said accusingly. "And when his marriage fell apart, you saw it as an opportunity to cover your tracks."

"Which was easy to do, seeing as you never once pulled the trigger yourself." Abraham once again assisted Tracker in breaking down the mayor. He continued where Tracker left off. "Ivan became a wanted man and you became mayor. Seems like an unfair trade, if you ask me."

"Where are you gettin' these lies from?" Mayor Jameson shouted, standing up in a fit of rage that knocked the cigar from his hand. The orange glow of the cigar was snuffed out as it bounced across the rug.

"Lucy Baker," Tracker revealed. "She told us just how much you tried to control your son and how you are still trying to control her. After hearing Lucy and the Reaper's side of the story, we are eager to hear yours."

"Clearly the two of you are incapable of seein' reason," the mayor snapped.

"Is that so?" Abraham crossed his arms and arched a thick brow. "Ivan was a little… unstable… but he could give us the details that Lucy was unaware of. Details that made it obvious they both came to the same conclusion."

"And what is that?"

"You ruined your son," Tracker answered. All the fight left the mayor's posture, and yet Tracker saw no remorse for his actions. It was clear Ivan had taken after his father more than he would have liked, for neither man showed any sign of guilt.

"I find these baseless accusations to be highly offensive," Mayor Jameson sighed. "But my son is not the reason you were asked to come here this evenin'."

Sheriff Walker stepped forward. He placed his hands on his hips and stood toe to toe with Abraham, although he was several inches shorter. Tracker knew his partner wouldn't back down, even if the verbal sparring turned into physical violence. And still Ranger Greene said nothing.

Tracker hoped Lucy had better luck searching the sheriff's home because they had gotten nowhere with getting answers from the mayor. To Tracker's utter shock, the tension drained from Abraham's shoulders. Tracker stared at his partner, shocked beyond belief that Abraham had not chosen to knock the lawman back with a well-placed punch.

"I'm sure you were busy helping the mayor with the preparations for the election," Abraham said instead. "That's why you weren't around when the solicitor was killed, right?"

Sheriff Walker squared his shoulders and replied with a single nod of his head.

Tracker felt his leg grow numb and hurried to stand up before the pins and needles set in. He wiggled his toes to keep the blood circulating through his extremities. "I knew Jeremiah Wilson," Tracker revealed. "He was a man with many flaws, but I enjoyed his company. And I will find out who took his life."

The sheriff finally squirmed under the weight of Tracker and Abraham's gazes. While it wasn't an admission of guilt, Tracker took it as a sign they were on the right track finally.

Chapter 11

Abe helped Tracker back to the hotel before he headed down to City Hall. He walked along the empty streets, watching as the townsfolk headed home for the night. A stale breeze helped dry the sweat that dampened the back of his neck. All seemed still, which only put him even further on edge. In a city plagued by ruthless outlaws, peace should have been a hard thing to find. However, it seemed people governed by a lazy sheriff and a worthless mayor had grown used to the rampant crime.

City Hall's doors opened, and Lucy greeted Abe on the front step., Neither of them uttered a word as she handed him a large envelope. Abe flipped open the flap and looked down at a bunch of handwritten letters. "Are these from Ivan Lincoln?" he asked.

"Some are from Victor. I recognize the writin'." Lucy pulled yet another parcel out of her satchel. "These letters are recent. Most of them talk about some sort of lock box. I thought it might be the so-called box of horrors Ivan mentioned."

"You got these out of the sheriff's home?" Abe questioned skeptically.

The brief smile that appeared on Lucy's mouth made his heart clench. She lifted a finger to her lips in a hush motion, as if what she said next was a secret between the two of them. "I got them from the mayor's house."

"It was risky going there alone."

"I didn't find anythin' at the sheriff's house," she said with a shrug. "Whatever is goin' on, I doubt the mayor would trust him with somethin' this big."

"Tracker mentioned Ranger Greene seemed just as surprised by the mayor's relationship with his son as we were. I might talk to him about coming clean about the mayor's illegal activities."

"I agree. Ranger Greene is a man of honor. He'll do the right thing." Lucy glanced over her shoulder at City Hall with a grimace. "But take a look at what happened in there before the undertaker cleans up."

"Is it bad?"

Lucy looked slightly green in the face as she nodded slowly. Abe looked up and down the road before he took her hand. Lucy wasn't the sort of woman who cared about the opinions of others, but Abe hadn't wanted to cause her any unnecessary strife. And telling by the way she lit up when he squeezed her hand, showing her a bit of affection had been the right choice.

"About our argument..." she started. "I'm sorry. Lettin' go of Ivan was—"

"This isn't the time, Lucy," Abe interrupted gently. He gave her a tight-lipped smile and pushed open the doors of City Hall. Flies buzzed around inside. It seemed like the stench of death had soaked into the walls. Dark stains marked the ground where Ivan had killed Jeremiah Wilson.

The stains were everywhere.

"Was he tortured?" Abe asked as he looked around with a queasy stomach. The man responsible for the murder was no broken-hearted son trying to get revenge on his father. Ivan Lincoln was a madman. No sane person could have butchered Jeremiah in such a way.

"I think so…" Lucy covered her mouth with a trembling hand to keep from losing her supper. She breathed deeply, reining control over her emotions. "Whatever happened… no human deserves to die like that."

Abe moved over to the largest of the dark stains. His eyes grew sinister as he tried to figure out just what had happened in that room. Boots tracked through the blood, creating a trail that led toward the back door. "He wasn't alone when he left," Abe revealed. "Two sets of footprints entered City Hall. The mud on Ivan and Jeremiah's boots made those. But look here."

Lucy squinted over at the footprints Abe pointed to. "These are three sets of boot marks… Looks like the blood caused them. Do you think it was Victor and the others?"

"Only one way to find out." Abe sighed as he moved toward the back entrance of City Hall. "Someone had to have seen something. I'll head down to the saloon—"

"We," Lucy interrupted. "We are heading down to the saloon. Together."

Abe nodded his head, but kept his mouth shut on the matter. With Tracker still injured, it meant Lucy was his only staunch ally in town. Ranger Greene and Sheriff Walker were still on his list of suspects until they proved themselves innocent. Abe had no tolerance for crooked lawmen. So he walked with Lucy down to the saloon.

Lively music streamed through the open shutters, mingling with the sounds of laughter from the patrons inside. Abe scowled when the music came to a sudden halt as he pushed through the swinging doors.

Lucy tucked her arm into the crook of his elbow, went limp, and slurred, "The night's still young, ain't it, fellas?" She gave Abe a secretive smile as the celebrations resumed. He was grateful for her quick thinking.

Abe lowered his head and helped Lucy over to the bar. The server's eyes lit up when they landed on her flushed face. If Abe hadn't known any better, he would have thought her drunken performance was genuine. "What can I get you, miss?" the bartender asked.

"A glass of your best wine and somethin' strong for my friend here." The sing-song tone of Lucy's voice rubbed Abe the wrong way, almost as much as her suggestive glances. He was no stranger to flirtation, but Lucy's actions filled him with jealousy.

"You look familiar, but I don't think I've seen your friend before," the bartender said.

Abe kept quiet.

Lucy lifted her hand to brush invisible wrinkles out of the bartender's shirt with a playful wink. "He's from out of town."

"That so?"

"I hear a lot of unfamiliar folks have come through here." She hiccupped. "If you believe the rumors, that is."

The bartender leaned closer to Lucy.

Abe clenched his hands into tight fists to keep from dragging the worthless fool over the bar and knocking him out cold. At least until he heard the bartender's reply.

"Well, I know the rumors are true," the man whispered. "Just a few days back, three or four men rode into town. People around here swear they saw the Reaper with them. The next mornin', they found that solicitor dead. That ain't no coincidence, if you ask me."

"Oh my!" Lucy clutched her chest dramatically.

Abe fought the urge to roll his eyes. He busied himself with his drink as she worked her magic on the bartender. From what he overheard, the men in question had definitely been Ivan Lincoln's gang. Abe didn't like what that implied. He knew if Victor, and the others had spent their evening in the saloon, someone else would have had to assist Ivan in Jeremiah Wilson's murder.

"What about Sheriff Walker?" Abe asked casually. "He heard nothing out of the ordinary."

The bartender's smile dropped, and his face morphed into a mask of confusion. "Actually, come to think of it, the sheriff was already outside City Hall when folks found the body. He said he heard a commotion inside and went to look."

Convenient, Abe thought.

"Who found the body?" Lucy asked before Abe had a chance.

The bounty hunter sat on the edge of his stool, fingers gripping the neck of his bottle hard enough to crack the glass as he waited for the bartender's reply.

***

Tracker hissed through his teeth as the stitches in his thigh pulled. He scooted to the edge of his cot, vision blurry as the room spun. Nausea bubbled up and left him with a sour sting on the back of his tongue. Tracker's unsteady hands reached for the pitcher of water on the bedside table. He poured himself a cup, brought it to his lips, and drank down the water so fast he thought he might explode from the pressure in his belly.

There was a knock at the door.

He set the cup aside and pulled his knife out of the sheath strapped to his belt. Tracker limped over to the door. "Who is it?" he called.

A mousy voice came from the other side of the door and told him there was a package delivered to the front desk. "Set it down and walk away."

Once the sound of retreating footfalls reached his ears, Tracker cracked the door open and picked up a small brown box. Abraham's name had been scrawled on the top, so he set it aside for his partner to find. Abraham often received packages from his sister or people they had helped in the past. Tracker turned around and...

A gentle breeze fluttered in through the window, fluttering the curtains. The window had been closed. Tracker had checked both windows in their room himself before Abraham left the hotel. He flipped the knife in his hand and crept closer to the bed. There weren't many places for an intruder to hide, and the bed was nearest to the window.

Bare feet shuffled across squeaky floorboards until he came to a stop near the corner of the bed. Tracker bent at the waist, careful not to tear his stitches, and grabbed the mattress with his free hand. He held his breath until the last possible moment before he flipped the bed over. Nothing. No silent killer awaited Tracker beneath the bed.

Scarred arms wrapped around his neck. Tracker was dragged to the floor as he struggled to wiggle free. His attacker held on like a viper. Searing pain radiated up Tracker's leg. He brought his elbow back, rammed it into his attacker's ribs, and then sliced at the forearms with his knife. He released him with a bellowing curse.

Tracker flipped to his feet and instantly stumbled. Blood trickled down his leg as he hobbled away from the attacker. He noticed the scent of gunpowder only seconds before a gun was leveled at his nose. "Whatever the Reaper is paying you…"

"I ain't working for the Reaper," the man revealed.

Tracker struck then.

He used all his remaining energy to knock the gun out of the man's hand. With a speed that often impressed his partner, Tracker lifted the blade of his knife and pressed against the jugular of his would-be killer. Shock and confusion rolled through him when he flicked open the button on the man's jacket and revealed a deputy's badge pinned to his vest.

"The sheriff sent you?" Tracker asked hesitantly. He would have expected a hired gun, an outlaw, or even one of the many drunk fools around the city, but a deputy? Tracker knew every man had his price. He also had hoped there were still some decent lawmen left in San Antonio. "How much is the Reaper's dog paying you for my head?"

"Not yours… Abraham Delaney's," the deputy sighed. "I was told to bring him in alive after I made it look like he killed you to cover up the solicitor's murder."

"Why?"

The deputy snorted. "Why do you think? Mr. Delaney goes down for the murders, and it looks like the sheriff was the one who captured him. Mayor Jameson appointed Walker as sheriff—"

"And taking down a rogue bounty hunter makes them both look good for reelection," Tracker finished for the deputy. "What about the Reaper? Where does he fit into this plan?"

The deputy opened his mouth to respond, but seemed to rethink his actions. Tracker tapped the other man's throat with his knife as a reminder. But the deputy wasn't alone. A second man appeared behind Tracker. Glass shattered over the back of his head, and he toppled over, crashing into the armoire in the corner of the room.

Tracker attempted to stand.

Both deputies sniffed the air. The scent of gunpowder was much stronger than it had been the first time Tracker noticed it. He struggled to peel himself off the pile of broken furniture and accidentally dropped his knife. The second deputy kicked Abraham's package onto the floor in front of Tracker's feet. "Open it," he ordered. "The darn thing stinks to high heaven."

Tracker reached for his knife and sliced through the braided twine holding the box intact. When the sides fell open, a loud click echoed through the room.

"It's a bomb!" Tracker shouted. Black powder trickled through an hourglass rigged to set off a stack of dynamite. He dashed across the room and dove out the window, hitting the ground with such force that he lost consciousness for several seconds. The only thing Tracker could hear was a sharp ringing in his ears. An intense heat forced him to open his eyes, and he looked up at a cloud of smoke as it engulfed the hotel in flames.

Chapter 12

"So… the deputies hired by Sheriff Walker found Jeremiah Wilson's body?" Abe asked the bartender, getting only a curt nod in return. Everything suddenly made perfect sense to him. Abe grabbed Lucy by the hand and pulled her out of the saloon. She could hardly keep up with him, but they made it outside, eventually.

"What's gotten into you?" she chuckled.

"When we first met, you said the men in town were too afraid to go after Ivan Lincoln," he said almost too fast for his own ears. "You said it was hard to find deputies after so many had been killed by the gang. Well… I don't think that's true anymore."

"You ain't makin' any sense."

"Sheriff Walker is double-crossing Mayor Jameson," he surmised. "The mayor thinks having the sheriff in his pocket will keep folks from finding out the Reaper is his son, but the sheriff realized he can make a little extra on the side by joining up with Lincoln behind his father's back."

"Ivan gives Walker men to work as fake deputies so he always has eyes and ears in the city." Lucy practically jumped out of her skin with excitement as she continued, "They pretend to be just as afraid as everyone else, so the real lawmen always have to go with Ranger Greene when he makes an arrest."

"Which puts them directly in the line of fire," Abe finished. "Mayor Jameson thinks his son is out to ruin his political career by terrorizing the town, but the truth is Ivan is just preparing to take over San Antonio. It's been his goal from the very beginning."

Lucy tangled her fingers with Abe's. "It's the perfect revenge. He gets to take back what his father stole from him and expand his so-called kingdom."

"This means Ranger Greene is nothing but a pawn in their fight for power." Abe glanced down the road, unable to meet Lucy's gaze. "We need to tell him what we learned before they get him killed."

The explosion knocked Abe off his feet. He threw himself onto Lucy, protecting her from the debris that fell all around them. Shrill screams filled the air. Abe waited until the dark spots in his vision cleared before he dragged himself to his feet. Lucy brushed off her blouse as Abe ran down the road in the direction of the fire.

"Tracker!" he shouted above the noise. Abe pulled the bandana from his back pocket and tied it over his mouth and nose as the thick smoke seeped out of the burning hotel. He scanned the faces in the crowd for his partner. "Tracker, answer me!"

A hand grabbed him by the arm just as he was about to charge into the flames. Abe spun around and nearly collapsed beneath the strength of his relief when he saw Tracker beside him. He could barely stand, and in fact, it looked like Tracker had been in a bare-knuckle boxing match and lost.

"The bomb was intended for you."

Abe took the news like a punch to the gut. "Who sent it?" he asked darkly.

"I was fighting off two deputies who said they were working for the sheriff," Tracker revealed. "They didn't recognize it, so it must have come from the Reaper."

He turned and looked up at what was left of the hotel's blackened walls. "How many people made it out?"

"Four people died, Abraham. There wasn't time to warn anyone," Tracker replied. "I should have known—"

"Don't." He forced Tracker to meet his gaze. "Don't go down that path. There have been times when I was on the edge of darkness, blaming myself for things I couldn't change, and you pulled me back. I have to be that for you now."

Abe draped Tracker's arm over his shoulder and helped him over to Lucy. She offered them a place to stay for the night, and both men were too tired to refuse. Lucy's home was small, with green shutters and white walls. She decorated the interior in soft hues of lavender and rose. It was all simple for a woman as complex as Lucy.

"I'll show you to your room," she said before she slipped into a corridor that was barely wide enough for Abe's shoulders. He supported most of Tracker's weight as he followed closely behind Lucy. She opened the door to the right, revealing a room that was far more masculine than the others.

"It was like this when I acquired the home," Lucy explained needlessly. "Make yourselves comfortable. I'll grab some bandages and put on a kettle."

Once Abe and Tracker were alone, Abe helped Tracker remove the deer hide trousers and vest that concealed his wounds. "This leg might be infected," he told his partner. "But it's better to be alive and sick than dead."

"Did you find anything at City Hall?"

"No. If anything, it gave us more questions than we had going in. We found the actual answers in the saloon." Abe repeated his theories to Tracker until the man had no energy left to keep his eyes open any longer.

***

Ranger Greene stood across from Tracker with his hands braced on the table. Tracker sipped the coffee Lucy had made well into the hours of the early morning, grimacing down into his cup as the cold sludge slid down his throat. Lucy and Abraham sat beside Tracker at the table. Abraham wore one of his famous scowls that put people on edge. The silence that had woven between the four of them chipped away at Tracker's patience.

"We need an answer, Ranger Greene," he said. "If we put an end to this, it will be with you on our side."

"You're certain they were Sheriff Walker's men?"

"I saw the badges, and they admitted it," Tracker replied. He felt like a train had run him down at full speed, but he was determined to see their investigation through to the end. "They helped the Reaper kill Jeremiah Wilson and then got him out of the city without anyone seeing."

Ranger Greene rubbed the back of his neck with a look of frustration on his face. "And Sheriff Walker has been his eyes and ears in this city all along… I'm embarrassed, gentlemen. I don't know why I didn't see this myself."

Tracker had wondered the same thing many times. Perhaps the criminals were too careful. Perhaps they had known just how to exploit the ranger's trust in the mayor. There were too many possibilities, and not enough people clapped in irons. Tracker respected Abraham's faith in the law, but Tracker was losing faith with each case.

"Worry about apologies and whatnot later. We need to find the man responsible for the bomb," Abraham said. "I went back last night and found some folks who were still trapped inside after they put the fire out. One woman was able to give me a description of the man who delivered the package to the hotel."

Tracker pushed against the table to stabilize himself as he stood up. He felt the blood drain from his face and fought to remain on his feet. "Then we should get going," he heard himself say, though his voice was rougher than usual. "Find the man responsible and make him tell us what the Reaper is planning next."

"You ain't going anywhere." Abraham placed his hand on Tracker's shoulder and forced him back in the chair. "Lucy patched you up, but you still need rest. Let me do the footwork on this one, and then we'll take Ivan Lincoln down together, all right?"

Shame burned deep inside of Tracker. "You check on the man who sent the bomb, but I will not sit here doing nothing." He then looked back at Ranger Greene and pointed at the lawman. "You and I are going to arrest the deputies who attacked me."

A red blush crept up Ranger Greene's cheeks. "I can't arrest them for attacking a Comanche... it ain't exactly—"

"I know," Tracker cut in. "But you can arrest them for acts of lawlessness."

"And the murder they confessed to a bounty hunter under the employment of Mayor Jameson," Lucy added before she gave Tracker an apologetic smile that scarred his pride.

Ranger Greene held his hands up to stave off anymore interruptions. "Fine. Tracker and I will question the two deputies while the two of you find the bomber."

Tracker didn't wait to hear what anyone else had to say. He grabbed his vest and pulled it on over the shirt Ranger Greene had lent him. Most of Tracker and Abraham's belongings had been destroyed in the fire that followed the explosion. What little they had left was barely enough to fill a single saddlebag.

The ranger walked beside Tracker as they left Lucy's home and ventured toward the sheriff's office. Neither of them spoke, even as the increasing discomfort in Tracker's body became more evident with each step. Sweat beaded on his forehead and upper lip. The dark circles rested beneath his eyes, and the blanched hue to his complexion was anything but flattering. He thanked his ancestors the walk was not a particularly long trek from Lucy's home.

"Let me do all the talkin'," Ranger Greene said as they reached their destination. "Right now, it's your word against theirs, and I want to make sure they slip up and reveal their plans."

"If you insist." He entered the sheriff's office after Ranger Greene. The two deputies he fought in the hotel room sat at a table cluttered with beer bottles, playing cards, and bullets. Sheriff Walker was behind his desk with a pen clenched between his teeth as he flipped through a file. The lawmen looked up at Tracker with smug grins on their faces.

To Tracker's surprise, Ranger Greene asked Sheriff Walker to leave the office while he spoke with the deputies. It was a daring move, one that shifted the balance of power between the men substantially. Ranger Greene was in charge. Tracker took pleasure in Sheriff Walker's misery as the man's smile disintegrated.

"What are you playin' at?'' asked the sheriff. "If you have somethin' to say to my men, then you can say it in front of me."

Ranger Greene snatched the file from Sheriff Walker's hand. "The recent development in the Reaper investigation requires my full discretion until we find out who is responsible."

"Nonsense."

"We have a witness who says he saw your men at the hotel last night." A bluff. Not a bluff with too much risk, but just enough misdirect that it forced the sheriff to keep his mouth shut. Tracker was impressed nearly as much as he was angry… but not quite.

Chapter 13

Abe entered the backroom at the saloon just as the sun set. He spent the entire day with Lucy, tracking down leads and asking questions. Their last witness sent them to the Branded Mare to find a man named Walter Jones. According to Lucy, Walter Jones was an alias used by Ivan Lincoln's right-hand man Victor.

They filled the backroom with cigar smoke.

Soiled doves sat perched on the laps of gamblers and other unsavory characters who filled the private area. Several of the men glanced up at Abe as he wove through the crowd. A woman with dark skin and short, curly hair brushed his arm. Abe smiled politely as he shrugged off her touch and continued toward the sofa. Four men hooted and hollered like they were wrangling cattle, paying the bounty hunter no mind until Abe stopped in front of a man fitting Victor's description.

"Wait a second... I know you—"

Abe dragged the outlaw out of his seat before he finished his sentence. Victor thrashed in his hold. Abe struck the outlaw in the jaw, causing him to crash into the cocktail table in front of the sofa.

Folks ran from the room screaming. The men with Victor stood up and dug for their guns, but Abe was faster.

He lifted his pistol and cocked it in the blink of an eye. "I wouldn't do that if I were you," he snarled. With a flick of his wrist, he gestured for the men to lower their weapons. "Nice and slow."

Victor pushed himself off the ground and wiped the blood from his lip.

"Abraham Delaney. My boss said you were reckless for a bounty hunter." Victor chuckled. "Only a madman would chance comin' in here alone."

"If your friends know what's best for them, they'll leave." Abe saw one man reach out of sight, and he lifted a second pistol into view. He smiled as the men gasped in awe at the speed of his draw. "I'll take all of you out before you can raise that gun to my chest, boy. Hands where I can see them."

"Do as he says!" Victor ordered.

The outlaws raised their hands toward the ceiling and backed out of the room. Abe kept one gun trained on Victor and the other gun trained on the men retreating from the backroom.

He holstered his weapons when he was alone with Victor. "What's Ivan got planned?" Abe asked in a very straightforward manner.

"You think I'll betray him?"

He punched Victor again, planting the outlaw flat on his rear end. "I won't ask you twice. Answer the question, or this will get a lot more violent."

"I thought you were supposed to be a man of the law," whined the outlaw.

"I'm a man of justice. Sometimes that means taking things into my own hands and putting a stop to cruelty." Abe straddled Victor and curled his fingers into the front of the man's bloodied shirt. "And you killed a lot of innocent people. I'm sure the law will forgive me if I turn you over with a couple of wounds."

"All right! Fine, I'll talk!" Victor's bottom lip trembled as he glanced around nervously. It was as if he was afraid of Ivan Lincoln appearing out of thin air. "He plans to kidnap the mayor and force the people to bow to him."

"How does he intend to make them bow?"

"Whatever it takes," the outlaw muttered. "That bomb was a warnin' to make you stay out of his way. Ivan wants to kill you himself, but only after he uses you to set an example."

Abe dragged Victor to his feet and wrenched his arms behind his back. The outlaw squirmed like a fish out of water, but Abe held him fast. He led Victor out the back door, where Lucy waited with the cuffs. She secured the outlaw's hands the second they stepped out of the saloon.

"We need to call a meeting with the mayor," Abe said. "I'll take him down to the jailhouse. You get the others, and we'll reconvene at your house."

"Be safe," Lucy whispered. She pushed up onto her toes and pressed a kiss to his stubbled cheek.

Abe watched her walk away with a strange stirring in his chest. He told himself it was nothing more than concern for her safety, but the truth of his feelings for Lucy was more obvious than he thought. Folks snickered quietly as they watched the bounty hunter stare after his lady like a lovesick pup. "As you were," he said, and cleared his throat.

Even Victor chuckled at Abe's expense, and that rubbed him the wrong way.

Abe forced the outlaw up the small steps of the jailhouse and shoved him inside one cell. "We'll see who's laughing when the people of San Antonio find out you were the one who blew up that hotel," Abe scoffed. "There's no way a judge will let you walk away a free man after something like that. I'm sure the survivors are looking forward to seeing you swing, Victor."

"Ivan will come for me."

Abe tossed his head back and laughed. "You betrayed him. All it took was a bit of pressure, and you cracked. Ivan Lincoln would rather see you rot in this cell than risk his life to save a man who turned on him. In fact... those men you were with are probably on their way to the Kingdom to tell him you talked."

The look of terror on Victor's face was nothing compared to the trauma he put his victims through. People had died because of Ivan Lincoln and his men. No matter what the mayor or Lucy believed, the Reaper had to face consequences for his crimes. Even if that meant the legend of Abraham Delaney was tarnished with the blood of an outlaw.

***

They passed bowls of stew around the table. Tracker thanked Lucy for her kindness and devoured his portion of the meal. His trust in her grew each day she remained by Abraham's side. Tracker had never seen his partner so content. He wondered whether some day that content might grow into happiness.

"I have to die," Abraham said suddenly, causing Ranger Greene to spit out his tea.

"What?"

"Hear me out," he said. "We can't attack Ivan on his own territory. That didn't end well for us last time. So we lure him here by telling everyone I'm dead."

"How do you suppose we do that?" Lucy asked irritably. Her nostrils flared as she squinted her eyes at Abraham.

Tracker bit back a smile as he pushed around lumps of potato in his bowl.

"We set a trap to arrest Sheriff Walker and his crooked deputies," Abraham explained. "With the letters Lucy found, the witnesses at the hotel, and the confession you wrestled out of them... There's more than enough evidence to justify an arrest."

Tracker nodded his head as realization dawned. "Walker will put up a fight."

"Exactly!" his partner said cheerfully. "It'll be a shootout, but it's nothing we can't handle. After they're in custody, we spread the rumor they killed me during the fight, and it'll reach Ivan before the day's end. News that big is bound to travel fast."

It was a decent enough plan, Tracker thought. Anything that turned the tides in their favor was welcome. The pain in his leg had finally subsided, and he looked forward to getting back into action. "It's almost time for the election," Tracker sighed. "Getting Sheriff Walker away from the mayor long enough to arrest him will be a challenge."

Ranger Greene scratched at his bearded chin and shook his head. "No. We got to make this public. Humiliate Walker in front of the people he swore to protect, and he'll snap."

"People could get hurt," Tracker argued. "They need time to recover from the fire."

But Ranger Greene disagreed once more. "The anger of the townsfolk will be added pressure. Might even be a riot when they hear the deputies did nothing to stop that bomb from goin' off."

Tracker disliked the thought of potential casualties, but he couldn't deny the ranger had a point. Grief and anger were powerful motivators. The outrage had the potential to cause enough chaos for Abraham's plan to work. "Fine. But what about the mayor?" he asked. "He is just as guilty as the lawmen."

"There's no evidence," Abraham replied. "Nothing to connect the mayor to the crimes other than Ivan Lincoln's word, and that alone isn't enough."

Lucy stood up from the table with an eruption of fury. Her chair toppled over, and her bowl of stew clattered to the floor. Thick, goopy beef stock slithered across the wood. "That ain't right," she shouted. "The mayor is the one responsible for all of this! Ivan wouldn't even be an outlaw if it weren't for his father. Are you sayin' that even if Walker and his men speak against the mayor at the trial... the mayor won't face charges?"

Abraham rested his hand on Lucy's arm to calm her anger. "Without evidence, it's all speculation. I'm sorry, Lucy, but the mayor is an innocent man in the eyes of the law. You're a hired gun in his employment... a court would see you as accountable more than the mayor."

Tracker winced as Lucy stormed out of the room. He understood her anger—the same problems had kept him awake at night. "Give her time," he said to his partner. "Miss Baker is a reasonable woman. She will see the truth of your words once she is no longer blinded by anger."

"Since when does Lucy have your vote of confidence?"

"She has put up with you for a month," Tracker jested. "I believe that would earn anyone my respect."

Abraham punched Tracker in the arm.

Ranger Greene cleared his throat, casting a look of mild amusement toward them as he arched a thick brow at their childish antics. "Can we get back to work, gentlemen?"

Tracker retaliated by kicking his partner under the table. "Yes, of course. Now that we have a plan, I think we need to find new deputies."

"Tracker's right," Abraham muttered. "Liberating San Antonio means we need people we trust to do the job Sheriff Walker refused to do."

"Sounds like you have someone in mind." Ranger Greene's gaze flickered between Tracker and Abraham, but both men hesitated. "Who is it?"

"Arthur Kent."

Tracker remembered Kent from a case they worked a while back involving a notorious outlaw named Corbin Frost. Despite having been raised by Frost, Kent turned out all right in Tracker's opinion. "Arthur Kent understands how outlaws think," Tracker said to support Abraham's suggestion. "He'll know how to deal with a mayor as crooked as Jameson."

"If he has your respect, then he has mine. Do you trust the men he travels with?" asked Ranger Greene.

Tracker chuckled under his breath before he answered. "The last letter I received from Arthur Kent said he found a travel companion in an old friend… Kary Delaney."

Chapter 14

One Week Before Election Day

The scent of hot coffee lured Abe out of a deep sleep. He opened his eyes just as a faint knock sounded on the door. "Come in," he called. After a few moments, Lucy shuffled into his room with a tray piled high with breakfast. Bacon, honeyed bread, eggs, and hash filled the bedchamber with a decadent aroma. "Lucy… this is…"

"I just thought you might want to start the day with a full stomach," she explained, with a coy smile on her lips. "And I wanted to apologize for the way I've been actin'. It just don't seem fair that Jameson still gets to be mayor."

Abe sat up with his back pressed against the wall. Lucy set the tray of food in his lap before she took a seat at the edge of the mattress. "I understand," he replied. "It took a long time, but eventually I learned justice and the law aren't always on the same page. Sometimes things just need to work themselves out, and people will get what's coming to them." Abe picked up a piece of bacon and took a big bite. The taste of salted pork coated his tongue. "It's delicious, Lucy. Thank you kindly."

Lucy chewed on her plump bottom lip and tucked a stray curl behind her ear. "Tracker said your sister should be arrivin' today with that man. I'm nervous."

"Why?"

"The way Tracker goes on about her sometimes, it's hard to imagine her likin' me," she said.

Tracker had never mentioned Kary more than a handful of times in Abe's presence. It was strange for him to think his partner had stayed in contact with both Arthur Kent and Kary, while Abe had failed to do so. In fact, Abe hadn't known Tracker and Lucy had grown closer during Tracker's recovery. Tracker kept very few friends over the years, and many were mere acquaintances rather than staunch allies.

"Kary has been through a lot," he said finally. "She would judge no one based on what they had to do to survive."

"If she's anythin' like you, I'm sure she's a wonderful person." Lucy remained by Abe's side as he finished up his food and then hurried back to the kitchen while he dressed for the day.

It excited Abe his sister agreed to join Arthur Kent while he transitioned into his role as the new sheriff of San Antonio. Kent also agreed to bring along six men he trusted to act as his deputies. Abe was grateful, for he knew the city needed all the help it could get. They desperately needed law and order in San Antonio.

With one last look in the mirror above the washbasin, Abe wandered out of his room to meet with Tracker on the front porch of Lucy's house. He stopped mid-stride just as he reached the door. "Did you… do something different with your hair?" Abe asked, looking at his partner with a skeptical eye.

"Yours would look better too if you washed it from time to time," his partner quipped. Tracker's braid was gone. His long locks were shorter than usual, coming to a stop just past his shoulders, and someone had shaved close the hair on the sides of his head. If his tawny complexion and muscular physique weren't enough to draw attention to his Comanche blood, the new hairstyle definitely would.

"Hey! I bathe every couple of days. I just don't see the point of making a fuss over my hair or the clothes I wear when I know they'll just end up dirty again in an hour," Abe grumbled defensively. "When does the train arrive?"

"It should be here."

Abe tipped his hat to Ranger Greene and followed Tracker toward the train station. A wave of folks from Virginia huddled on the streets like lost sheep. There were two kinds of people who moved further west, far away from the hustle and bustle of the big cities: the ones who had no choice but to seek a new beginning and the ones who had everything they needed and still wanted more.

"There they are," he heard Tracker announce.

Abe looked at the passenger car and spotted his sister in the crowd. Arthur Kent's sharp gaze seemed to miss nothing as he escorted Kary off the train. Abe greeted his sister with a smile, pulling her in for a warm embrace. Kent and Tracker shook hands before Kary launched herself into Tracker's arms. The sheer shock of the moment left Abe speechless. Tracker set Kary aside, careful with placing his hands, and put a respectable distance between them.

Abe saw the burning flush on his partner's face and tugged his sister aside. "What on earth is going on, Kary?" he hissed.

"Don't you take that tone with me, Abraham Delaney. I'll remind you which of us is the older sibling." Kary flicked open a fan and used it to cool herself off in the summer heat. "And—while it is none of your concern—I must admit that Mr. Tracker and I have been corresponding—"

"Kary," Abe snapped to cut his sister off. He lowered his voice to a whisper. "There can be nothing between you and Tracker, hear me? Your stubbornness will get a good man killed."

His sister glanced over her shoulder at Tracker as a wistful expression appeared on her face. "I don't care what you have to say, Abraham," Kary sighed. "I intend to ask Tracker to come away with me… to a place where we can be together without fear."

"It's nothing but a fool's dream, Kary." Abe reached out to stroke his sister's cheek. "The two of you have suffered enough in this lifetime. Don't go causing trouble where there is none."

She flinched away from his touch and turned back to grab her things. Abe watched as Tracker took Kary's bag from her hands and carried them back to Lucy's in silence. It was clear Tracker was still very cautious about his interactions with Kary, while she had thrown caution to the wind. Abe just hoped it prepared his sister to fight for what she wanted. Kary was resourceful, but society had its own way of breaking dreamers.

***

"On my signal," whispered Ranger Greene as he crouched beside the front entrance to the sheriff's office.

Tracker moved to flank the door with Abraham. His long, serrated blade was out of place among the many guns his partner and the lawmen carried. It glistened in the sunlight as heat rippled up from the ground. Sweat dripped down the sharp point of his nose before it dripped onto his moccasins.

Ranger Greene gave them the sign to push forward.

Tracker kicked the door to the sheriff's office open, causing splinters of wood to fly across the room. He moved left as Abraham moved to the right. Ranger Greene and Kent rushed down the center with their guns drawn.

"Hands toward the sky!" Abraham yelled. "Thomas Walker, Gideon Nile, and Jeffery Goodwin, you are under arrest."

Walker jumped from behind his desk and grabbed a shotgun off the wall.

Tracker dove toward the floor, narrowly avoiding a fatal shot. He crawled on his belly over to where Abraham had taken cover. The new deputies the mayor hired with Kent and Abraham's recommendation surrounded the building. There was nowhere for the former lawmen to go except into a cell.

But that hadn't stopped the criminals from putting up a fight.

Goodwin fired his rifle, and the bullet grazed Ranger Greene's shoulder. Abraham hurried to the ranger's side and used the bandana from his back pocket to tie off the wound and stop the bleeding.

Kent's pistol was knocked out of his hand. The new sheriff dodged a hit from Nile. Tracker spotted a hidden weapon in the former deputy's hand. He leaped to his feet and sent his knife soaring through the air. The blade hit Nile in the arm just as a small revolver came into sight.

"Thanks," Kent shouted with a wide grin.

Tracker gave a nod of acknowledgement just as Nile clutched his wounded hand and curled his lip at the new sheriff's badge pinned to Kent's vest.

"We ain't done nothin' wrong!" the criminal barked.

Tracker ignored the outburst and pulled his knife from Nile's arm. Kent wrangled Nile into one of the small cells in the sheriff's office.

Another blast from the shotgun sent Tracker racing for cover once again. He rolled across the floor and came to a stop behind the wall, where the wanted posters were stapled to a plank of wood. He was at a disadvantage within the small confines of the sheriff's office. There was barely enough room to hold a conversation, let alone a bow and arrow. But Tracker stayed out of Walker's line of sight as he inched toward Goodwin—the one he recognized from the attack at the hotel.

Goodwin fumbled as he attempted to reload his firearm. The former deputy was too slow. Tracker struck the man in the jaw and held him at knifepoint. "This feels familiar," Tracker said. "I remember being in a similar situation before the hotel blew up."

"Yep. I knew I should have put a bullet between your eyes that night." Goodwin turned his head and spat obscenely onto the floor with a snort. "You got nothin' on us. I'll be out by the end of the day."

Tracker smiled as he stepped aside to allow Kent enough room to lock Goodwin in the cell with Nile. "We shall see," he taunted.

A loud noise and a cloud of black powder sprayed Walker in the face as his shotgun misfired. The former sheriff stumbled out the back door, only to be surrounded by the new deputies. A small crowd had formed outside, but Kent's men kept the townsfolk at bay. They looked on as Tracker tackled Walker to the ground. He pressed his knee to the former sheriff's back and secured his hands.

Ranger Greene helped Tracker place Walker and the others in one cell while Kent assisted with the last steps of the plan. Abraham traded clothes with one of the new deputies with a similar build and then carried the deputy out like a lifeless body. Though it was nothing more than trickery, Tracker had trouble looking at the fake body that looked so much like his brother in arms.

"You got no reason to arrest us," Walker wheezed. "We're innocent! This is a gross abuse of your authority."

Tracker gripped the bars with both hands and leaned forward. "We have witnesses that place your deputies at the hotel during the explosion."

"And a confession from the barman at the saloon who has sworn to speak at trial and tell the judge you were involved in the death of Jeremiah Wilson," Ranger Greene added smoothly. "But I think it will be the handwritten letters between you and Ivan Lincoln that will sway any judge. Our good friend Lucy Baker was kind enough to supply us with the most crucial evidence against you."

Tracker couldn't help but grin when he saw the dumbfounded expression on Walker's face. They had been so careful, so cunning, that Walker must never have expected to get captured by the law. Cold satisfaction settled inside of Tracker. They finally caught the men who had attacked him and failed to protect the people of San Antonio. He stared down at the once-proud lawmen who sat on the dirt-covered ground with their heads bowed in shame.

"You should smile," Kent snickered. "The three of you will be legends in a couple of hours. After all, only the best could kill Abraham Delaney."

Chapter 15

The wagon stopped outside the saloon. Two deputies passed by just as Ivan reached for the flaps of the wagon cover. He held perfectly still until they were out of sight. The moment his boots touched the ground, Ivan noticed the city had a different atmosphere.

People walked along the sidewalks with their heads bowed. Even children looked absolutely dejected as they sat on the front steps of their homes. Ivan frowned as he pushed his way inside the saloon. "Where's Victor?" he asked a young bartender, who polished the glasses with a rag. "He was last seen in this establishment."

The bartender set the glass aside, swung the rag over his shoulder, and leaned over the bar. "Abraham Delaney arrested Victor," the young man whispered. "Ranger Greene had him transported to Dallas the very next mornin'."

Ivan cursed quietly and scrubbed a hand over his face in frustration. "What's with all the gloom around here?"

"Didn't you hear?"

"Would I be asking if I had?" Ivan snapped. It was obvious the kid didn't recognize him, but he had very little tolerance for stupidity.

"The old deputies and Sheriff Walker were arrested, too," stammered the bartender. "There was a big fight just three days ago. They shot Abraham Delaney dead, and folks are waitin' to show their respects at the funeral."

Abraham Delaney is dead?

Even though Ivan wanted the bounty hunter dead, his mind seemed to reject the notion a legend like Delaney had ended so abruptly. Folks practically worshipped the ground he walked on. It was no wonder the entire town was in mourning. "Who's the new lawman around here?" he asked suddenly.

The kid looked rather nervous as he backed away from the counter and fussed with another glass. "That's Sheriff Kent. Arthur Kent."

"*The* Arthur Kent?" Ivan couldn't believe his ears. It wasn't too long ago Kent was a man on the run just like him. How he became sheriff of a growing city like San Antonio was beyond Ivan's comprehension. The whole situation had Abraham Delaney written all over it. "Where's the Comanche?"

The bartender shrugged and carried on with his work. Ivan dropped a bundle of cash onto the counter, causing the young man's eyes to widen like saucers.

"That's for the suite upstairs and... your full discretion, of course." He slid the cash over and waited for a reply, foot tapping impatiently.

"Right away, sir." The young man added some money to the register and pocketed the rest.

Ivan gestured over his shoulder. "Bags are in the wagon outside. Make sure you handle them with care," he said. Ivan then walked up the curved staircase, along the upper gallery, and down the corridor. He stepped inside the suite with a sigh, noting the few differences in the room since he last stayed in the city. But even if the room had been the same, the city itself had changed. The fear was gone.

Ivan moved deeper into the room and braced his hands on the windowsill. Wind fluttered a tendril of hair that fell over his forehead, carrying the scent of horse and sweat from the people who wandered the streets. They had blocked a few areas of San Antonio off for construction, but otherwise the city writhed with life. From somewhere behind Ivan, the young bartender dropped the bags on the bed.

"Before you go," the outlaw began. "I must ask one last favor from you."

"Sir?"

"I need you to give a message to Lucy Baker over on Kindling Road," he instructed. "Tell her Ivan wishes to invite her to supper at the new eatery to express his condolences in person."

"Right away, sir."

The young man shuffled from the room and closed the door. Ivan was left alone with his thoughts. It was uncertain whether Lucy would accept his invitation, but he hoped beyond reason she might. Out of everyone, Lucy never gave up on him. It was Lucy who had defended him at every turn, even if she knew in her heart he was guilty.

Ivan still loved her. He had mourned her death years ago, only to find out she had been alive all along. With Abraham Delaney out of the way, Ivan had one last chance to win her heart and stake his claim on the city that shunned him. There were only a few men left in his gang, but he had a plan that was sure to succeed.

Ivan heard a knock at the door and closed the shutters. He walked over, opened the door to his suite, and grinned when he saw his men. They tipped their hats before sitting down on the sofa near the extensive wardrobe. Jerry, Angus, Jasper, and Wade were quieter than usual, and that didn't sit right with Ivan.

"One of you better speak up or I'll make you," he growled.

Wade removed his floppy old hat and cleared his throat. "Boss, we were just thinkin' that Victor might have talked."

"Victor wouldn't do something like that."

"But how else did Walker and his boys get caught?" Jasper asked. "I mean, either Victor talked, or they did."

Ivan shook his head and leaned against the wall with his arms crossed over his chest. "It don't matter. We stick to the plan and get my father out of Texas so I can kill him myself across the border. I can't become mayor after he's gone if I'm wanted for murder."

"You're already wanted for murder..." Wade said with a confused frown.

"No," Ivan snorted. "The Reaper is wanted for murder. No one will question when Jameson's long-lost son returns to take his father's place as mayor. Which means we'll have to get rid of Ranger Greene as well."

Ivan disliked the skeptical looks on the faces of his men. Ivan stood before them and lifted his arms in a grandiose pose. "I'm the king of outlaws," he boasted. "And I have not been held captive or persecuted in nearly a decade. Now is not the time to doubt me. Now is the time for us to take what these hypocrites call a civilized society and make it our paradise. Abraham Delaney's death marks the start of a new era."

***

Four miles outside San Antonio, Texas

Abe sat beside a rolling stream, enjoying the faint mist of cool water that dampened his face and neck. Out in the open field, with his back propped up against a tree that provided shade, Abe could escape the noise of the city. There were three days until the election. Three days for Ivan Lincoln to attempt to abduct the mayor.

"I was wonderin' where you disappeared to." Lucy's sweet voice drifted to his ears, and Abe couldn't help the surge of joy that rushed through him. He cracked open his left eye to get a look at Lucy as she sauntered over to his tree. Her wild curls and flowing skirts billowed in the wind.

"I needed to think," he replied.

Lucy knelt on the ground beside him. "Your sister was worried. She seems to believe you might do somethin' reckless."

Abe shrugged and reached over to pluck a dandelion from the patch of grass beside his leg. "She might be right," he huffed. "I can't stop thinking Ivan will slip through our fingers and we'll lose our last chance at catching him."

A vibrant blush colored Lucy's cheeks while she toyed with a loose thread at the cuff of her dress. "He contacted me. That's why I came to find you," she explained. "Ivan is in the city, and he wants me to meet him for supper."

Abe sat up straight and looked Lucy in the eye. "It could be a trap. Promise me you won't go…"

She hesitated for a second, chewing at her bottom lip nervously. "Ivan and I have nothin' to talk about," Lucy answered. "I promise I won't see him… but I've questioned some things."

He was relieved that Lucy's affection—or pity, maybe— for Ivan had dwindled. "What sort of questions?"

"About you and me."

Abe felt his heart race. "I've thought about us as well," he admitted. "But you have to understand I never saw a future for myself that included a wife or family."

Lucy gasped. She grabbed Abe's hand and chuckled. "One thing at a time. No one said anythin' about startin' a family just yet. I just… I want you to know I've grown to care for you. I think I might be in love with you, Abraham Delaney."

Abe cupped Lucy's cheek with one hand and pulled her closer to him with the other. "We would have to walk away from this life, put all the violence behind us, so that we could live a proper life," he said. "Hang up our pistols and become civilized people."

"But it would be worth it! Startin' a new life with you will be all the adventure I need." Lucy nuzzled her cheek against the palm of his hand. "But what about Tracker?"

Abe wasn't sure how to answer her question. He stroked along her jaw with a calloused thumb, marveling at the softness of her skin. "Tracker will do whatever he pleases," Abe said eventually. "He'll always be welcome in my life, but if he wants to move on, I won't stop him. For many years, he was the only family I had. I'd be sad to see him go."

Lucy gave Abe a mischievous smile and pressed a kiss to his lips. Abe was frozen in place. Whether it was because of the softness of her lips or the shock of her brazen actions, he didn't know, but he savored the taste of her kiss long after she pulled away.

"What was that for?" he asked, voice raspy from desire.

"I'm a good-for-nothin' mercenary, Mr. Delaney," Lucy teased. "I make my own rules."

He reached out for her, but Lucy leaped back and dashed toward the little stream beside the tree. Abe watched as she tossed her boots aside and waded into the shallow waters. Lucy pulled her long curls aside and beckoned Abe closer with a crook of her finger. He snatched his boots off, tossed them aside, and rolled up the bottoms of his trousers before he met her in the stream.

"You're more than just a mercenary," Abe whispered as he pulled Lucy into his arms. "And when this is over... I want you to be my wife."

Tears glistened in her beautiful blue eyes. Lucy jumped into Abe's arms, catching him off guard. They fell back with a big splash of cold water. Lucy delighted as Abe coughed and sputtered like an ornery brute. She peppered his face with little kisses. "Of course I'll marry you, Abraham!" she squealed happily, splashing around in the water. "Only a fool would turn down such an offer."

"I haven't asked you yet," Abe snorted.

"My answer is yes! I can't wait to tell Kary and Tracker and—" Lucy paused suddenly. She crawled into Abe's lap as he wiped the water from his face, not caring one bit that her sodden skirts tangled around them. "The world thinks they have killed you. I want to shout to the peak of the tallest mountain that I'm Abraham Delaney's girl, but I can't."

He pecked her on the tip of her nose. "This will be over soon," Abe sighed. "Until then, you can run along and tell my sister."

Abe collapsed with a burst of laughter as Lucy shot off like a bullet back toward the city. He trudged out of the water, gathered their things, and whistled for his mount. "Are you going to run all the way back to San Antonio?" he called after her.

"I'm so excited that I just might!"

He shook his head and climbed into the saddle. Water dripped onto the dry ground beneath the horse, but the old stallion seemed quite happy with the cool water along his back. Abe rode up next to Lucy and yanked her up into the saddle with him.

Chapter 16

Construction at the hotel was slow, but Abe did what he could under the cover of night. When the city was quiet and everyone closed their shops, he climbed a ladder to the roof and worked until sunlight peeked over the hills. The bomb that destroyed the hotel had been intended for him, and he felt obligated to do most of the work. San Antonio was a beautiful city with a bright future ahead of it without Ivan Lincoln causing trouble. Abe thought the least he could do was to repair the damage he was responsible for.

"I believe congratulations are in order," Arthur Kent said from below. "Though I think your bride might have a problem with you spending your nights out here instead of with her."

Abe smiled to himself and hammered in one last shingle. He gripped the ladder, eased his way down, and turned to face the new sheriff. "We aren't engaged just yet, but I've stated my intentions," he replied with a touch of amusement. "What's keeping you up tonight?"

Kent rubbed the back of his neck, turning his head to stare down the empty road. "You really got me in a mess this time, Abe."

"I know."

"Even after we get rid of that coward, this city will have to be reformed," Kent grumbled. "I don't know who here can be trusted, and I don't like feeling like I have to look over my shoulder now I'm a free man."

Abe nodded. He walked beside Kent, back toward the sheriff's office. It was rather quiet after Walker and they sent his boys to the jailhouse under the watchful eye of Kent's deputies.

Abe pulled a chair over to the sheriff's desk and propped his feet up as Kent took the other seat.

"You sound like you have a plan," Abe said. "Mind sharing it?"

"If a lying mayor and crooked lawmen weren't enough to worry about, Tracker said Jeremiah Wilson's hands weren't clean either." Kent removed his hat and leaned back in his chair with an exhausted sigh. "I'm wondering just how deep the rot is. What's next? Bankers? Dressmakers?"

"I'm sure you don't have to worry about Mrs. O'Donnell getting into trouble." Abe chuckled. "But I understand your concern."

"I want to send a letter to Chicago."

The statement took Abe by surprise. He wondered why Kent seemed so distraught over the idea. "Send a letter to whom?"

"The Pinkertons," Kent replied. "I have looked everywhere I can think of trying to search for that box Lucy goes on about."

Abe knew where Kent's thoughts were headed. "I suppose you reckon that, if you find the box, you can get to the root of the corruption and use it to take down Jameson."

"Getting rid of the mayor will send a message to the rest of them," said Kent. "It'll show this city that the law won't be taken lightly now that I'm in charge."

"Then what's the problem?"

Uncertainty entered Kent's gaze. The sheriff fumbled with a drawer and pulled out a file. "The Pinkertons were the reason I was a wanted man in the first place," he confessed. "Some distant relatives of mine had hired them to find me after I went missing as a child. Corbin Frost kept me well hidden in his gang. Leaving to save Kary was what put me in their sights. They had no choice but to report me to the authorities when they identified me. Still..."

"That sort of dirt isn't easy to wash off," Abe muttered sympathetically. "Being associated with Frost tarnished your name, made you a criminal in the eyes of society."

"Thanks to you, that isn't the case anymore." The smile on Kent's face was genuine. Abe felt the comradery from across the desk. "But I figure if anyone can hunt down that box of Jameson's, it'll be them."

The door opened just as Kent finished. Kary entered the sheriff's office with Tracker trailing at a respectable distance.

Abe quirked a questioning brow at his sister. "Why are the two of you out and about this late?" he asked suspiciously.

"Lucy made you supper, and I told her I would make sure you ate it." Kary set a basket on top of the desk and pulled out a bowl and spoon before handing it to Abe.

"And Tracker?"

"I was making sure she arrived safely," his partner answered.

Kary, however, seemed opposed to the idea. "And I told him I didn't need his protection." She lifted the long skirt of her dress to show the small pistol strapped to her ankle. "Old habits die hard, I suppose."

"Kary," Abe growled disapprovingly. "You promised to put all that behind you if I allowed you to help with this job."

"I know, I know." She waved her hand dismissively and filled his bowl with lamb and potatoes. "It's just a precaution. Besides, it's Lucy you'll have to worry about."

Once again, Abe found himself smiling at the mere mention of Lucy's name. "I know she causes trouble. She said as much the first day we met when I woke up in a cell. But it's the outlaws who should worry about Lucy."

Kent laughed as he cleared the papers and files from his desk. "That woman sure knows how to make a man regret his actions. Best not anger your future bride, Abe. It might not end well for you."

"No," he snorted. "I don't suppose it would." Abe picked up his bowl and ate every last bite as he thought of Lucy. She meant the world to him, and he had only known her for a short time. He wondered just how different his life would be if he hadn't met her at all. He was grateful Jameson was a yellow-bellied coward and a liar—otherwise Abe might not have punched the mayor and ended up in that cell.

***

The back door to the church swung open, and an older man held a lantern up to shine a bit of light onto Tracker's face. He held his breath as he waited for the preacher to call for help or slam the door in his face—after all, the history of his people in Texas was painted red with the blood spilled from many battles. But he saw no fear in the preacher's gaze. There was only concern.

"What can I do for you, child?" asked Father Michaels.

Tracker revealed the Reaper's intentions to take the mayor hostage and their plan to put a stop to the outlaw's wicked deeds once and for all. Father Michaels listened closely, offering nothing more than a simple nod or frown where it was appropriate to do so. Tracker spoke until he was forced to stop for fear of losing his voice.

"I understand we are asking a lot of you, but it is with good intentions."

"You want me to lie to my congregation and hold a false funeral in my church for a man who is not dead?" Father Michaels questioned.

"We are asking you to make a sacrifice to help save this city and the lives that will be lost if you do nothing," he answered. "I have heard your god is forgiving. I'm sure he will understand one small lie to save hundreds of lives."

Father Michaels hesitated for a few seconds more, but he eventually lowered the lamp and shook Tracker's hand.

The following day, Tracker heard the bells ringing to welcome all to the Sunday morning sermon as he walked along the perimeter of the church. As expected, the people of San Antonio gathered inside to join the preacher in prayer. Tracker had visited Father Michaels at dawn and asked that Abraham's funeral take place after the first sermon of the day, and the man of God had agreed begrudgingly.

Tracker scanned the faces in the crowd as he crept inside behind them. They crammed half the city inside the small church. Songs were sung, donations given, and passages read from the Bible. The words spoken in honor of Abraham's life were beautiful, despite the dishonesty of his death. Tracker was more than grateful his partner was still alive and well.

He continued to search the many faces in the crowd, and he did not waste his efforts. Seated in the third row was Ivan Lincoln. The self-proclaimed king was flanked by two men who matched the descriptions Lucy had given him.

Tracker spotted the telltale bulge of a pistol on each of the men and cursed under his breath. The calculated expression on the Reaper's face made the knot in Tracker's stomach tighten. He hurried out the door and climbed on the back of his mare.

Kent's deputies watched from afar as Tracker rode toward Lucy's home. He cawed like a crow to signal that they had spotted the Reaper in the city. Hooves thundered against the dry dirt road. Dust filled the air, stinging Tracker's eyes as he pulled back on the reins.

Kary Delaney rushed to the front door when his horse approached. "What is it?" she called. "What happened?"

Tracker threw his leg over the saddle, lowered himself to the ground, and hitched his mount to the fence in front of the house. "I saw him. The Reaper is here in San Antonio."

"Where is he?"

"At the church with two armed guards," Tracker answered. "No one seemed to recognize him."

"Lucy said he's been careful to keep his identity a secret." Kary held the door open for Tracker.

He passed her on his way into the house, holding his breath as his shoulder accidentally brushed her arm. It was second nature for Tracker to flinch away, but the hurt in Kary's eyes made him regret it. "I do not mean to offend you," he whispered, making sure his words were for her ears only. "It's best if we remain cautious… at least while we are here in Texas."

Something akin to hope appeared in Kary's blue eyes, and it terrified Tracker. He swallowed thickly and opened his mouth to speak once more.

Thankfully, the sound of footfalls came from the stairs. Tracker feared he might have said something foolish if they hadn't been interrupted. Ranger Greene came around the corner and stepped into sight. "I heard the signal. What happened?"

"I saw the Reaper."

"The election is tomorrow. This can't be a coincidence," said the lawman. "I'll have Kent and his men double security. You and Abe need to find somewhere to hide the mayor."

Tracker pulled the preacher's message from his pouch. "I met with Father Michaels earlier, and he agreed to hold the mayor in the church if there is an emergency."

"Tracker, I hate to ask this of you," Ranger Greene began. "But we need someone at that saloon to keep an eye on the place tonight. Ivan liked to stay there in the past and—"

"Of course. I'll go right away." Tracker nodded his head and went to pack his bags for the night. He felt Kary's eyes on him at all times, and shivered. She liked to hover in doorways or sit down on the chair in his room just to watch him. They rarely spoke more than a handful of words to one another, but she seemed content just to share his space.

"You don't always have to put yourself in danger," she whispered. "It doesn't always have to be you. Someone else can go."

"It has to be me."

Kary stepped in Tracker's way. She crossed her arms and stared up at him with tears in her eyes. "Because you see your life as less valuable than theirs?"

"Because being near you makes me reckless." Tracker gently nudged Kary aside and eased into the corridor. He walked back down the stairs, out the front door, and toward the saloon without sparing a glance over his shoulder.

Chapter 17

Election Day

The scent of gun oil clung to Ivan's fingers as he cleaned and polished his rifle. He watched through the window as people flocked to the large stage built at the center of San Antonio. The entire city was abuzz with excitement, and Ivan couldn't wait to wipe the smiles from their pathetic faces.

"Soon, boys," he said. "Soon this city and all her treasures will be ours."

Jerry picked at his teeth with a long, dirty fingernail. "So let me get this right," the outlaw slurred. "We kill the mayor in Mexico, and the Reaper disappears forever. Then you return as Ivan Lincoln with a big speech about mendin' your father's mistakes and fixin' the crime problem in the region. And after you're sittin' pretty in the white mansion at the top of the hill, us outlaws are in charge? You think these folks are dumb enough to fall for it?"

"I know they are." Ivan set his gun aside and pulled on his coat. "I've peeked behind the veil, gentlemen. I have seen what it's like in the world my family fights to keep alive, and I'm telling you men like my father are a dying breed. Lineage, legacy, and respectability mean nothing. We're bringing back the ruthlessness, cold-hearted honesty, and rebelliousness that founded this great nation."

"Old money don't last forever," Jerry replied. "Your father lost sight of what was important when he became mayor."

Ivan brushed off his hat as he gazed over at his men. "The people have forgotten who they are. They've grown fat and content while so-called heroes like Abraham Delaney spit false gospel about justice and liberty. Well, where was our justice when the world decided our way of life was no longer acceptable?" He fitted his hat to his head and grabbed his gun from the table. "Let's remind them that the land they stand on was won by rulebreakers!" he continued. "Let's deliver them into our kingdom of true freedom."

His men cheered. They holstered their weapons and rushed to the door with their masks pulled into place. Ivan took one last look out the window as a carriage rolled up to the stage. He saw his father—appearing as if he was larger than life, even from far away—walking up the small steps with the new sheriff and Ranger Greene beside him.

Hypocrites. All of them are hypocrites, Ivan thought to himself with a sneer.

He pulled his scarf up and concealed the lower half of his face. Anger burned inside of him, growing stronger with every step he took closer to the door. Ivan didn't leave through the back door or the saloon's entrance like his men. He located the door that led to the terrace and scaled down the side of the building, landing with a quiet thud near the small corral.

Ivan moved through the throng of people on the street with his rifle heavy against his spine. He lowered his head, using the shadow cast by the brim of his hat to keep the scarf around his mouth hidden. They posted deputies at the surrounding buildings, with two sharpshooters on the roof. Ivan had wanted to believe Victor's loyalty had not been shaken. But doubt had set in as he realized the lawmen were expecting him.

Ivan wove his way between people who acted like mindless sheep, clamoring for the attention of a man who had thrown his own son to the wolves. Jameson cared for no one but himself. Ivan only wished his father had choked on his own lies a long time ago. Lord knew he had been force-fed pointless speeches about expectations and duty. It seemed not much had changed as his father approached the podium to address the crowd.

"I would like to take a moment to thank you all for your unwavering support," said the mayor. City officials stood beside him: treasurers, managers, and council members dressed in their best garb to impress the masses. But no one was foolish enough to run against Jameson for mayor. It didn't matter whether they were aware of just how far the man will go to protect his status. In the eyes of his precious city, Jameson was a paragon—an icon of power and intimidation.

Ivan lifted his hand and squeezed his fingers against his palm in a tight fist. Gunshots rang through the city, cutting the speech short as people scrambled for cover. Outlaws and hired guns stormed the stage, but an arrow struck Ivan in the shoulder.

He searched high and low for the Comanche. "Come out, you coward," he shouted from behind his mask. "Face me like a man!"

"He's gone," Jerry hollered. "The mayor's gone, boss!"

A shadow of rage darkened his vision. Ivan gripped his rifle and shot down one sharpshooter on the roof. His men opened fire on the crowd, scattering the horde as they hunted down the deputies one at a time.

"Find him!" Ivan ordered. "Tear this city apart until you find him."

He tore the arrow from his shoulder and tossed it aside. His gaze landed on Ranger Greene. Ivan leaped over the side of the stage, rushed the Texas Ranger, and bashed him in the face with his rifle. Ranger Greene stumbled back, found some cover, and reached for his revolver. Ivan squeezed the trigger, shooting at the lawman until he was out of bullets.

"Where is he?"

"You're done for, Reaper," the ranger cackled above the gunfire. "You'll never find him. We've made sure of that."

Ivan reloaded his rifle with his back pressed against the wall of the bank. He clenched his jaw as he breathed heavily through his nostrils. "My men have you pinned down, Ranger. It isn't over for us yet," he claimed. "How long do you think you can hold on to that pride of yours? We'll kill as many people as it takes to bring you to your knees."

***

Tracker moved quickly.

He grabbed the mayor and forced him low to the ground. His sharp gaze was trained on the church as he navigated his way through the stampede of people trying to escape the gunfire. Mayor Jameson followed obediently, his large body hunched over to stay out of the line of fire. Tracker cut down an outlaw that blocked his path. His hands moved so fast the criminal's eyes widened in shock before he crumpled to the dirt.

"Keep moving," Tracker whispered to the mayor.

They reached the front of the church just as chaos erupted near the stage. Father Michaels allowed them inside, and Tracker slammed the door behind them. Deputies moved the pews to barricade the door. Abraham and Lucy stood near the altar with their guns in hand.

"Talk to me, partner," Abraham said. "How bad is it?"

"The Reaper's gang is killing anyone who stands in their way." Tracker helped close the shutters on the windows as he spoke. "I have seen a lot of terrible things, Abraham, but nothing like this. They will be slaughtered if we do not fight back."

"How's Kent... and his men?" Abraham asked nervously.

"They were pinned down when I got the mayor. Ranger Greene is fighting the Reaper on his own," he explained. "We must help them."

Abraham picked up a large sack from the ground and pulled out several firearms. Tracker watched as his partner tossed rifles, shotguns, and pistols to the men in the church. "Father Michaels, is there any place you and the mayor can hide?"

"There is an emergency crawl space beneath the floor," stammered the preacher.

"The two of you need to get down there and stay quiet. I'll have two deputies stand guard." Abraham moved toward the back door. "The rest of us will fight."

Tracker, Lucy, and Kary readied their weapons. They followed Abraham out of the church and through the alleyway between the church and Father Michaels's house. Kary broke off from the group when they neared the center of town. She climbed up onto the roof of the bank with her rifle. Tracker resisted the urge to go after her. He knew Kary could take care of herself, but the thought of her getting hurt nearly sent him over the edge.

Abraham tapped Tracker on the shoulder, disrupting his train of thought, and pointed to a very large outlaw who stood nearly seven feet tall. Tracker could tell by the loom on his partner's face that Abraham had no intention of fighting the colossal criminal.

"No," Tracker argued. "Why do you always make me fight the big ones?"

"I thought you liked a challenge."

Tracker jutted his thumb in the man's direction. "That is not a challenge. That is a mountain wielding an axe."

Abraham popped his head out from behind his cover. He winced as the enormous outlaw pummeled one of Kent's deputies. "I think you can take him," Abraham said unconvincingly.

Lucy rolled her eyes and ran toward the brute. Tracker watched in awe as she climbed the outlaw like a tree and punched him in the head repeatedly. Abraham ran to defend his woman, but Lucy shot him a look that stopped the bounty hunter in his tracks. No matter what the outlaw did, he couldn't seem to shake Lucy off his back. Tracker would have found the whole thing amusing if he hadn't been grabbed from behind.

He gripped the forearm that attempted to crush his windpipe and flipped his attacker over his shoulder. Tracker wrestled the man to the ground. He hit his attacker in the throat so hard it forced a gust of air out of his mouth. Another outlaw appeared in front of Tracker, and he threw his knife. It spun through the air until it lodged in the outlaw's stomach.

Tracker sprinted to the area behind the stage. Ranger Greene was injured and bleeding badly as he leaned against a wall to keep his balance. The lawman's face was completely drained of color. "Ivan is holed up in the saloon," Ranger Greene said. "Kent chased him down."

"Don't talk. Can you make it to the church?" Tracker asked.

"I think so."

Tracker shoved himself beneath the ranger's arm and helped him reach the end of the block. They moved behind the buildings, trying to avoid the Reaper's gang. When the church was in sight, Tracker handed Ranger Greene off to a deputy and returned to Abraham. "I know where the Reaper is," he said to his partner.

Abraham stayed out of sight and knocked one outlaw unconscious. "Where's Kent? He needs to be there to make the arrest."

"He chased the Reaper to the saloon," Tracker said. "Let's go." He led Abraham down the sidewalk and felt sick to his stomach by the number of innocent people killed by the ruthless outlaws. Tracker had never seen so much carnage. He was surer than he had ever been that Ivan "the Reaper" Lincoln deserved an arrow between his eyes.

Abraham stopped Tracker with a hand on his arm. Just through the front doors of the saloon were four armed guards. The Reaper stood behind the bar, with Kent held hostage at gunpoint.

"Rushing in will get Kent shot, and he deserves better than to die at the hands of a man like Ivan Lincoln," Abraham said. "Let's do this my way."

"If it goes badly, then we end it my way." Tracker pointedly reached for his bow and pulled an arrow from his quiver. If Abraham could not talk the Reaper down, Tracker was prepared to take matters into his own hands.

Chapter 18

Tension coiled deep in the pit of Abe's stomach. Too many bullets were flying for his comfort. They had to find a way inside without risking Kent's life. He stayed crouched as he moved along the side of the saloon. A single outlaw guarded the back door.

"Stay here," he mouthed to Tracker.

Abe dug his fingers into the dirt, freed a rock from the earth, and tossed it to break a window in the building to the left of the saloon. The outlaw stepped out of the doorway to look, and Abe snuck up behind him. One hand covered the outlaw's mouth while the other gripped his throat tightly. He clung until the man lost consciousness.

Tracker helped Abe lower the outlaw to the ground, and the two bounty hunters slipped into the saloon unseen. Abe approached the first door along the hallway and used his gun to push his way inside. He let loose a sharp exhale, as every nerve in his body tingled with awareness.

"Where did Ivan find all these men?" Abe asked Tracker.

"I assume most of them are hired guns."

He recalled Ivan Lincoln's gang being rather small, so Tracker's assumption must be correct. Like his father, Ivan seemed to inspire loyalty in others, even if it was undeserved. Abe wondered whether Ivan might have made a decent mayor if he had embraced his father's vision. But

Abraham had learned the hard way that a father's love was often full of good intentions, yet destructive.

Kary's presence was a constant reminder Abe's own father had made some poor decisions. Decisions that had led Abe to that very moment, torn between what was right and what was easy as he stepped back into the corridor. The hall that led to the parlor was quiet. Abe recognized it from the night he arrested Ivan's man, Victor.

Abe stood tall as he approached the doors of the parlor. He dropped his pistol to the floor and nudged it with his boot. The gun slid across the floorboards with a metallic scrape as he entered the room. His arms lifted toward the ceiling. Beams of sunlight spilled over his shoulders, casting an amber glow within the parlor.

Ivan Lincoln's eyes widened with realization. "You… it can't be," the outlaw gasped. "They buried you."

"They buried a casket full of stones." Abe took another step closer and heard a gun cock. He paused mid-stride with his stormy blue eyes on Ivan Lincoln. "It was the only way we could make sure you would come."

"Faking your own death was clever… but what now?" Ivan asked. "What other surprise does the great Abraham Delaney have in store for me?"

Abe lowered his hands to his sides. He never once looked away from Ivan, not even when he sensed the other outlaws getting closer to him. "Your father is safe," he replied. "So is Ranger Greene, Lucy, and so many others you've threatened."

Ivan waved his gun at Kent. "Who is he to you? What makes him so special you would risk your life to save him?"

Abe shook his head with a sigh as he concluded men like Ivan Lincoln were too far gone to see reason. He pointed to Kent and said, "Let him go, and you can take me."

"And do what exactly?"

"You can do what you do best," he replied. "You can run. Having me with you will keep the sharpshooters from pulling the trigger."

Ivan shoved Kent aside and approached Abe. "What's keeping me from shooting you right now?"

"Me," said a voice Abe knew all too well. Tracker fired arrows into the parlor.

Abe dived for Kent and rolled to the other side of the bar. He pulled the gag from Kent's mouth and used his knife to sever the ropes that bound the sheriff's arms.

"When did that partner of yours get so reckless?" Kent grumbled. "I think it's a vast improvement."

Abe snorted as he searched for a way out. Tracker's distraction wouldn't last forever. "I'll lay down some cover fire, and you make a run for the swinging doors," he told Kent, but the man was too stubborn to listen.

Abe watched as Kent fired aimlessly at the outlaws. Ivan's gang took cover. Bullets punched holes into the tables and surrounding furniture until it covered the ground in a layer of wood dust.

The doors opened with a loud bang. Lucy held two pistols in her hands as she unloaded the rounds. Ivan crawled across the floor to where Abe had kicked his pistol. The bounty hunter jumped on top of the outlaw's back. They struggled for the gun, landing sharp punches against each other's bodies in the skirmish.

Abe's back hit the floor. Ivan pulled the trigger, and a bullet splintered the plank of wood right beside Abe's head. He bucked Ivan off, trying to blink away the sting of gunpowder in his eyes as his ears throbbed painfully. The click of an empty chamber just barely reached his attention. Abe tackled Ivan, and they broke through a door. Bruised knuckles battered the outlaw's face.

Ivan shoved Abe to the side and made a run for it. Abe wobbled as he climbed to his feet. He limped after Ivan, rounding the corners of the hallway until he came upon a bedchamber. Ivan stood just barely inside the room. The outlaw glanced over his shoulder menacingly.

There was nowhere to run.

The saloon was all that kept the sharpshooters on the roofs from taking that fatal shot. Abe had the outlaw cornered. "Make this easier on yourself," he huffed in wild, gasping breaths. "Surrender to Sheriff Kent, or his deputies will make sure you don't walk away from this."

"I know information..."

Abe shook his head. "It doesn't matter anymore," he replied. "Kent hired the Pinkertons to investigate your father. It's only a matter of time before they find the truth."

"Fifteen men," he said. "That was all it took to turn this city into a battleground." Ivan lowered his scarf and wiped a trail of blood from his lip with a wince.

Abraham Delaney's watchful eyes tracked his movements.

Ivan wondered what the enigmatic man had on his mind, but he didn't care enough to ask. The pain in his shoulder from the arrow kept him from wandering too far from the present. "You're protecting a man who doesn't deserve it."

"Jameson isn't my problem," Abe grumbled. "I signed a contract to capture you and deliver you to your trial *alive*, and that is what I intend to do."

Ivan chuckled to himself and pulled the scarf back over his mouth. The fight wasn't over. Though he had lost most of his men in the first wave of violence, so long as there were people willing to fight for his cause, all hope was not lost. He picked up the vase from the vanity and tossed it at Abe. The heavy blow knocked the bounty hunter off balance, and Ivan used the distraction to climb out the window. He used the route he had taken earlier that morning, shimmying down the wooden beam that supported the terrace. His hands burned from the friction, but he didn't let it stop him.

Bullets hailed down upon him as the sharpshooters took turns trying to put him down. Ivan dodged every one of their gunshots with zigzag movements. Sweat cascaded down his face like a waterfall, soaking into the scarf that still concealed his identity. He slid to a stop and rounded the corner at the edge of the city, only to get hit in the chest with a plank of wood.

Ivan struggled to breathe as he looked up into the eyes of a woman he never met. Her features were familiar and yet foreign all at once. "Who the hell are you?"

"Kary Delaney," she said with a sarcastic curtsy.

Ivan rolled onto his feet, despite the pain that rattled in his chest. He reared his arm back and went to knock the woman unconscious. She dodged his swing with skill, jabbing her fist into his ribcage, and he had a creeping suspicion she was toying with him. Ivan dropped his guard, knowing the woman would attack. When she tried to hit him again, Ivan grabbed her arm and twisted it behind her back. He used Kary Delaney as a shield as he moved toward the stables.

Her frustration was palpable. "You won't get away."

"Perhaps not," he replied honestly. "But I don't plan on dying today."

Tracker ran toward them like a bull at the rodeo. Ivan held Kary closer to his chest and watched a deadly inferno blaze in those untamed eyes.

"How sweet," Ivan chuckled. "Forbidden love is always the strongest, isn't it? I like to think I had that with my Lucy."

"Lucy never loved you," Kary hissed.

"Now that's just a hateful thing to say." Ivan yanked her arm a bit harder, causing her to let out a squeal of discomfort that put Tracker on edge. He reached down to her hip and pulled the pistol from her holster. "You won't be needing this."

Abe, Lucy, and Kent closed in on him from all sides. But Ivan wasn't alone. Four of his men approached with their guns drawn.

"Let my sister go," demanded Abraham Delaney. "Let her go, and I'll cut you a deal."

"She means nothing to me." Ivan released the woman with little thought.

Freed from the threat of immediate danger, Kary rolled onto her back and kicked him in the leg. His knee buckled.

Chaos erupted as Abraham Delaney and his allies collided with the outlaws. Ivan punched Abe in the throat and grabbed the gun from his hands before shooting the man in his side. Ivan's own injuries affected his fighting, but the blood pumping through his veins gave him a burst of reckless courage. His gang was outnumbered now, and they were losing. He grabbed Lucy and pressed his gun to her head.

Abe froze when Ivan pulled back on the hammer.

"Kill him, Abraham!" Lucy ordered. "End this now before anyone else gets hurt."

And Ivan could tell Abe wanted to obey. But he knew the bounty hunter would not risk the woman he loved.

Abe let his gun drop to the floor.

Ivan assumed he won and shoved Lucy aside and opened his mouth to speak, but Abe rushed him. Both men crashed through the stable doors. What remained of his gang tried to go after them, but gunshots sprayed the side of the building as the lawmen fought to keep the outlaws at bay.

Ivan dug his thumb into the hole from the gunshot in Abe's side, causing him to shout in pain. The bounty hunter worked up enough strength to knee Ivan in the gut. They rolled away from one another. Abe clutched a hand to his side as Ivan hopped on his uninjured leg.

Bullets peppered the ground near Abe's boots, and he ran toward the back of the stables. Ivan appeared behind him and smashed Abe's head against the wall. Abe landed a punch to the man's ribs before he stomped on the outlaw's injured leg.

Ivan picked up a shovel and swung for Abe's head, but the bounty hunter ducked out of the way. The move allowed Abe to evade the attack, but it knocked him off balance. His breath came in angry pants as he swayed on his feet. Abe called his name from somewhere far away, but he couldn't make out the words. All the pain in his body slowed his movements, and yet he continued to swing the shovel hoping to hit the bounty hunter.

Abe feigned to the left just as Tracker opened the stable doors.

Ivan was hit so hard that his vision blacked out for a few seconds. When he came back to awareness, Abraham Delaney disarmed him with a flourish of his hand. The warm muzzle of a pistol pressed against the underside of his chin. And Ivan couldn't help but smile.

He dropped to his knees before his enemy and lifted his hands in surrender. "You win," Ivan said. "You've conquered greatness, Mr. Delaney."

Chapter 19

Tracker's bow was knocked out of his hands.

He hit the dirt and grabbed the pistol from the outlaw's boot. He looked up and took a shot, hitting the outlaw in the hand to disarm him. Ivan's men were outnumbered now. Three deputies were dead, one injured, and another one looked ready to bolt if a single bullet came his way. But they had beaten the odds, and Tracker was proud to fight beside them. Ivan's men must have noticed the change in the way he fought, for they made a run for the stables.

Tracker fired, and the bullet hit one man in the leg.

The colossal outlaw who fought against Lucy returned to the fray. He had impeccable reflexes and grabbed one of the uninjured deputies to use as a shield. "Guns down, boys, or I shoot him dead!" shouted the outlaw as he cocked his pistol and pressed it to the deputy's temple. "I know you don't want his blood on your hands."

Tracker clenched his jaw, and his nostrils flared with disgust. He hated cowards. "There is nowhere for you to go," Tracker replied. "Killing him solves nothing."

"It means there's one less lawman in the world, and that's all right by me."

Tracker dropped his gun and attempted to follow Abraham's example when Lucy and Kary attacked the large man at the same time. Kary snatched the gun from the outlaw while Lucy tripped him, but neither of them was strong enough to fight the mountainous man. Tracker pushed his way in front of the outlaw and a powerful kick landed against his chest, causing him to go flying backward.

He smacked into a saddle rack and felt one of his tender ribs fracture. Tracker was on his feet much faster than he expected. His head spun dangerously as he kept the outlaw from reaching the women. Kary fought off another outlaw as Lucy helped Kent hunt down the rest of the gang as they tried to escape.

"You should not be in this fight," he shouted at Kary.

"Then give me a reason to stay away." Her words were playful even as she dodged one punch after another.

Tracker landed a vicious blow to the outlaw's back, causing the man's knees to buckle. "What sort of reason would you accept?" he asked.

"Run away with me."

Suddenly, a sound exploded within the stable. Kary and Tracker shared a look of concern before Tracker shoved the outlaw away from him and ran for the stable doors. The outlaw seemed to have a similar idea. Tracker didn't want the outlaw to assist the Reaper, so he tackled him to the ground and pounded his fists into the outlaw's face. His vision blurred, and the anger that had been brewing inside of him since they signed the contract in the canyon valley overflowed. Tracker dug his fingers into the mud beneath him and pulled out a rock. He bashed the outlaw in the head with the stone, trying to knock him unconscious.

Each swing took more energy than the last. He missed because of the pain that came in nauseating waves through his body. Tracker's strength faltered, and he looked down at the battered face beneath him. He could have killed the man and avenged all the innocent lives that had been lost that day. But something divine kept him from crossing that line. Tracker knew, if he continued, he would lose himself to the anger—he would have been no better than the outlaws he fought against.

Kary took the stone from his hand and pressed a kiss to his bloodied knuckles. "Come back to me," she whispered.

For a moment, he allowed himself to feel the warmth of her touch. He banished the guilt and the turmoil... but only for a moment. Tracker snatched his hand away. He stood up and hobbled toward the stable doors. Mud and murky red stains covered his clothing. Tracker pushed open the doors and caught sight of his partner. Abraham took the gun from his target, and Ivan "the Reaper" Lincoln dropped to his knees.

But the happiness Tracker should have felt never came, for he watched his partner fall to the ground with his hand clutching his side. Tracker realized then just how badly Abraham had been injured. Kent pinned the outlaw to the floor of the stables and secured his hands with iron cuffs as Tracker moved to help his partner. Abraham blinked slowly, matching the rhythm of his faint pulse, and Tracker feared the worst.

Kary let out a scream so devastating it reached into the deepest recesses of Tracker's soul. He swallowed the pain and nausea that threatened to consume him and lifted Abraham off the ground. Lucy held Kary as she wept, but her eyes spoke of a sadness too great to ever comprehend. And though the world had already mourned the loss of Abraham Delaney, Tracker did not stop walking until he reached the doctor's office. It was no surprise people ignored him.

The doctor worked hard to assist the people of San Antonio in the aftermath of Ivan Lincoln's attack. It was a nurse who spotted Tracker and recognized Abraham. She waved him inside, instructing Tracker with firm words that fell upon deaf ears. One minute, he stood at the center of an infirmary, and in the next, he sat in a chair across from the cell where the Reaper gasped for breath. "I hope you pray to your god for death," he heard himself say. "And I hope it lingers just out of reach. You deserve the pain of a thousand deaths."

The Reaper scoffed with a grimace. He inhaled sharply and rasped, "I... am death. And the only... soul I come to claim... is that... of Abraham Delaney."

Epilogue

Five Weeks Later
Dallas, Texas

The church was washed in radiant light as the guests milled in through the doors. Everyone was on their best behavior after Kent threatened to lock people in cells if they ruined Abe's wedding. Abe wasn't big on the whole idea of marriage or the typical wedding traditions, but he had agreed to do things the way Lucy had always dreamed. Father Michaels had explained to Abe that marriage took sacrifice, and there wasn't a price Abe wouldn't pay to make Lucy happy.

Sure, they still bickered from time to time, and perhaps that was why he loved her. He felt no pressure to pretend around Lucy.

There—in Father Michaels's office near the back of the church—Abe lowered a hand to his side as he looked at the hideous scar in the mirror. He traced the line with the tip of his finger, marveling at just how much damage one bullet had done. Autumn had finally arrived and the Pinkertons had located enough evidence to remove Mayor Jameson from his position. A trial was still underway, but it was yet another piece of good news for the people of San Antonio. Ivan Lincoln had gotten exactly what he deserved, and those who aided in his crimes were punished equally.

Though he had been forced to retire, he looked forward to seeing the coming changes to San Antonio. The city was on its way toward rebuilding. It wouldn't be long before they found a new mayor.

After all, hunting outlaws was easy. The fear and excitement that came with knowing he would spend the rest of his life with Lucy was indescribable. Abe felt as if he could take on the world.

The door opened with a whoosh, and Tracker hurried inside, with Kent beside him. They stripped off their coats and grabbed the tailored suit jackets that had been set aside for them.

"Are you sure you want to do this?" Kent asked. "Folks around here aren't used to this sort of extravagant wedding."

"It's what Lucy wants." Abe's smile fell when he saw the look on Tracker's face. "What is it now? Don't tell me there's bad news."

"Not exactly," Tracker hedged. "With you and Lucy settling down here, I'm leaving Texas with Kary. Being together here is not an option and—"

Abe punched Tracker right in the jaw. He shook his hand as his knuckles cracked, furious when the blow barely caused Tracker to wince. The healing was slow after he got shot by Ivan Lincoln, and the knowledge his body would never be the same didn't help his confidence, but Tracker should have at least asked for his blessing. "You know how I feel about you and Kary running away like a couple of lovesick teenagers," he grumbled. "But I suppose it isn't the worst thing the two of you have done. Besides, if this is the only way to keep my sister from being a mercenary… I reckon I have to be all right with it, don't I?"

Tracker smiled and pulled Abe in for a tight hug. "Thank you, brother."

"You better send a letter as soon as you find a place to settle down, you hear?" His entire body protested, but he allowed them this moment for as long as he could manage. Abe shrugged out of the hug and took his partner's hand. "I'll miss you, Tracker."

"I will miss you as well, Abraham."

"All right. Let's get this over with so I can finally have some peace of mind." Abe sighed as he walked into the chapel with his friends by his side. He waited impatiently for Lucy, fidgeting with the cuff of his suit, until the church doors opened. Abe felt his heart stop the second his eyes landed on her.

Lucy walked down the aisle in a powder blue dress with blonde lace around the cuff and the bust. The fabric looked soft, but even the beauty of the garment paled compared to Lucy. The flush of her cheeks bewitched Abe and the auburn curls piled atop her head whimsically. He took her by the hand as the preacher began the ceremony. Her lush lips mouthed, "I love you," and suddenly it was hard for him to breathe.

Abe wasn't sure just how far into the service Father Michaels was, but he pulled Lucy against him and kissed her with a passion few men had been blessed to experience. Kent whistled, and the congregation cheered them on as the preacher looked down his nose at them in disapproval. But Abe didn't care about any of that. He stared into the bluest eyes he had ever seen and wondered how his dreams had become a reality.

The End

Would you consider leaving a review on Amazon? I would appreciate it.

More westerns are in the works.

www.ingramcontent.com/pod-product-compliance
Lightning Source LLC
Chambersburg PA
CBHW071619150726

48000CB00004B/1797